Canine Detective Chris

The Shiba I...
Tracks Down the ... Jewels!

Tomoko Tabe

Illustration by **KeG**

New York

① Tomoko Tabe

Translation by Stephen Paul ❖ Cover art by KeG

TANTEIKEN CHRIS Vol.1 SHIBAINUTANTEI NUSUMARETA HOSEKI O OU!
©Tomoko Tabe 2020 ©KeG 2020
First published in Japan in 2020 by KADOKAWA CORPORATION, Tokyo.
English translation rights arranged with KADOKAWA CORPORATION, Tokyo through TUTTLE-MORI AGENCY, INC., Tokyo.

English translation © 2023 by Yen Press, LLC

JY
150 West 30th Street, 19th Floor
New York, NY 10001

Visit us at jyforkids.com • facebook.com/jyforkids • twitter.com/jyforkids
jyforkids.tumblr.com • instagram.com/jyforkids

First JY Edition: December 2023
Edited by Yen On Editorial: Emma McClain
Designed by Yen Press Design: Lilliana Checo

JY is an imprint of Yen Press, LLC.
The JY name and logo are trademarks of Yen Press, LLC.

Library of Congress Cataloging-in-Publication Data
Names: Tabe, Tomoko, author. | KeG (Illustrator), illustrator. | Paul, Stephen (Translator), translator.
Title: Canine detective Chris / Tomoko Tabe ; illustration by KeG ; translation by Stephen Paul.
Other titles: Tanteiken Chris. English
Description: First JY edition. | New York, NY : Yen On, 2023. | Audience: Ages 8-2 | Audience: Grades 4-6 |
Identifiers: LCCN 2023039013 | ISBN 9781975378646 (v. 1 ; trade paperback)
Subjects: CYAC: Dogs—Fiction. | Courage—Fiction. | Detective and mystery stories. | LCGFT: Detective and mystery fiction. | Light novels.
Classification: LCC PZ7.1.T27 Can 2023 | DDC [Fic]—dc23
LC record available at https://lccn.loc.gov/2023039013

ISBNs: 978-1-9753-7864-6 (paperback)
       978-1-9753-7865-3 (ebook)

10 9 8 7 6 5 4 3 2 1

LBK

Printed in the United States of America

Canine Detective Chris

**The Shiba Inu Detective
Tracks Down the Stolen Jewels!**

Hinata Kurihara

A shy fifth-grade boy who's very kind and loves animals.

Chris 🐾

A Shiba Inu and former police dog. Chris is brave, except when it comes to bugs!

Mayuka Yoshizawa

Hinata's childhood friend. Bright, bubbly, and full of energy.

Shunya Oomori

Hinata's grandfather, a dog trainer.

Officer Iwata

A policeman who works at the local police station.

Suzune Kurihara

Hinata's mother, a veterinarian.

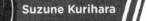

Contents

Takaki Moriyama

A college student who lives in the area.

Sakurako Shimazu

Owner of Sakura Jewelry.

Rui Takeuchi

Hinata's classmate.

The First Case

Christie the police dog sat proudly with his chest puffed out.

"All right! Let's go, Christie," said Kobayashi the trainer, holding the leash. "Do it like we practiced, and you'll be fine." Christie's brown tail wagged a little.

That day was Christie's first job—his proud debut as a police dog. Christie and his trainer were in the parking lot of a shopping mall near the port. It was late afternoon on a spring day, and the air was still cool.

Kobayashi turned to one of the plainclothes investigators next to him and asked, "Is this the suspect's car?"

"That's right. We got a tip that the stolen goods were being handed off at the mall, but apparently, they found out we were onto them, and they took off. This was in the driver's seat."

The investigator handed him a sealed plastic bag. Kobayashi took the bag, pulled out a single work glove, and held it before Christie's nose.

Sniff.

Another investigator watched Christie smell the glove and remarked, "Kind of rare for a Shiba Inu to be a police dog, isn't it?"

"Yes, usually they're German shepherds. But this one's excellent. He passed the police-dog test with almost full marks."

Christie stopped sniffing the glove and looked up at Kobayashi.

"Okay, search!"

The dog immediately put his nose to the ground and began to pace around, tracking the scent. Kobayashi and the investigators followed behind him.

"We looked all over the area but couldn't find anything. There's a big crowd, after all…"

Despite it being a weekday, the parking lot was busy, and there were lots of people coming and going.

Kobayashi nodded. "For places like these, it's better to have a smaller Shiba than a full-size shepherd. Not only are they easier to get around with, but they don't frighten as many people."

The investigator nodded, impressed.

Kobayashi was a small man with a kindly face, and he was dressed in casual attire and a windbreaker. He and Christie simply looked like a young man and his dog out for a walk.

Members of the public would never dream that he was actually an officer out patrolling with his police dog.

Christie followed the remaining scent, growing more certain with every step. He left the lot and went toward a street. While one of the investigators stopped traffic, the police dog marched directly across the road and turned left along the wharf overlooking the water.

When Christie reached the end of the wharf, the dog finally lifted his nose from the ground and looked at Kobayashi with concern.

"Don't worry," he said. "You can find it. Keep searching."

Christie pointed his nose into the air and sniffed around. Kobayashi and the investigators watched with bated breath.

Eventually, Christie stepped onto a patch of grass to the right, poked eagerly through the greenery, then resumed walking.

"Hmm, he's heading to the pier...," observed one of the investigators.

Crossing over the grass to the pier was quicker than following the path.

The other investigator remarked, "Wait! That's it. The handoff of the stolen goods didn't happen at the mall. They did it on...a boat?"

The dog confirmed his suspicions by heading straight down the pier.

"Look!" the investigator cried. A small cruiser at the end of the pier was just starting up its engine. A man on board hurriedly undid the rope tying the boat to the dock.

Both of the investigators took off running, shouting, "Stop that boat, right now!"

The suspect jumped behind the helm, just as one of the investigators grabbed the end of the rope. The cruiser's engine roared to life, pulling the boat away from the pier and yanking the investigator into the water. His partner reached for him, only to be pulled in as well.

"Aah! Oh no!"

Kobayashi started running, too. Christie practically pulled him off his feet, rushing toward the end of the pier.

Suddenly, however, the leash went taut, and Christie was yanked backward. Behind him, Kobayashi was lying facedown on the ground. And behind Kobayashi was a man holding a metal pipe, breathing heavily.

Instantly, Christie rushed back to Kobayashi's side.

"C-Christie, here…"

He reached out, offering something in his hand to Christie. The dog took it into his mouth as Kobayashi undid the leash before shouting, "Go, Christie! Don't turn back! Just run!"

Christie hesitated for only a moment, then hurtled between the pipe-wielding man's legs and sprinted away.

"H-hey, wait!" the man shouted. Christie zipped back up the pier and leaped into the grass.

In the distance, a sound like a third splash could be heard, but the Shiba Inu paid it no mind and kept running, just as Kobayashi had ordered.

After bursting out from the grass, Christie nearly ran into some officers who had come walking over from the mall.

"Christie? What's this?"

Christie came to a stop, growling softly as the policemen approached.

"Hey, his leash is off. What happened to Kobayashi?"

The officers shared a confused look. Christie started to back away.

"Did something happen down there?" asked one of the policemen, pointing toward the pier. At that moment, a bug took flight from the grass and grazed Christie's snout.

Feeling itchy, Christie lifted up his paw to rub his nose—and promptly yelped.

"Yiiiiip!"

Here Comes Chris!

Hinata rushed home excitedly, his backpack bouncing with each step.

I can't wait to read the book I checked out! he thought, scrawny arms holding a large and heavy book—but he didn't mind the weight at all.

Now that break had ended, he'd stopped by the school library for the first time in a while and found a really neat treasure: a photo book full of some of the world's most interesting and rare creatures. It was a gold mine for any kid who loved animals as much as he did.

"Hee-hee… I can't wait to take my time looking at every single page!"

Hinata practically skipped along, flinging his feathery hair up and down. Until recently, he had dreamed of becoming a veterinarian, like his mother. But the more he gazed at the vivid photographs of animals in the book, the more he liked the idea of becoming a photographer instead, traveling the world and visiting exotic places. He decided he was going to save up his allowance until he could buy a camera.

After crossing the train tracks beside Aoba Station, he headed into the nearby shopping area.

The street wasn't that busy, and the way was narrow—just big enough for two cars to pass each other, but it was the only place in the neighborhood where you could buy most things you needed. There was a little supermarket, a drugstore, a bakery, and a deli with fresh food. There were even Chinese and Italian restaurants.

Hinata's home wasn't too much farther. He was holding up the book, rubbing his cheek against its cover, when someone smacked his backpack from behind.

"Hinaaata!"

Hinata spun around in surprise and saw his classmate Mayuka Yoshizawa, from Class 5-1, standing there with her hands on her hips. While she was short and slim, she held a boundless energy in her small frame. Her hair was done up in pigtails fastened with red hair ties.

"What's with you, Hinata? You look like a goofball," she remarked.

Hinata quickly wiped the smile off his face and composed himself.

Mayuka had been his friend since kindergarten. Their families were close, and because they were both without brothers or sisters, they were raised almost like siblings. She was one of the few people whom shy, reclusive Hinata could talk to without worrying about what she thought. Still, he felt a bit embarrassed that she'd seen him grinning to himself like that.

"N-nothing," he replied. "I just found a neat book, so I was a little excited."

"Uh-huh…"

Her sharp eyes peered at the item he had clutched in his arms.

"That looks really heavy," she said. "Is it a book about animals?"

"Yeah… What's wrong with that?" He turned away to hide his treasure from Mayuka's prying eyes.

"Nothing at all. I know you love animals. Let's get going so we can look at it together!" she said, grinning and grabbing his arm.

"What? T-together? I wanted to take my time reading it by myself!"

As Hinata tried to shake off Mayuka's grip, a voice nearby said, "Oh, aren't you two so sweet? Take care on your way home."

It was Sakurako Shimazu, the owner of Sakura Jewelry, a small store in the area. She was polishing the glass door of her storefront with a soft towel as they passed by.

"Oh! Good afternoon, Miss Sakurako," said Mayuka

happily. Hinata nodded slightly at the woman.

Sakurako was well over seventy years old, but she was very lively and fashionable. She ran the jewelry store all on her own.

"That's a really pretty scarf," Mayuka said.

Sakurako lifted a hand to her collar and beamed. "Thank you, Mayuka. It was a present from my son. Just perfect for early summer, isn't it?"

"Exactly the kind of tasteful gift I would expect from a jewelry designer!"

"Of course, he's so busy with work that he hardly ever visits anymore. I guess that makes sense, though. He has a job at a major jewelry company, after all," Sakurako explained, looking wistful.

Mayuka pursed her lips. "He should quit that job and help you run *your* shop instead…"

Sakurako shook her head. "The problem is, my business is so small, it could go under at any moment."

"But it's such a special place! I love looking at your displays out front. Once I grow up and get a job, I'll come and buy some jewelry from you. Hang in there until then!"

"Thank you, Mayuka, that's very sweet. I'll be waiting," Sakurako said, smiling. "Hinata, say hello to your parents for me. Tell them Latte is doing very well, thanks to them."

Latte was the name of Sakurako's Chihuahua. They were a tiny light-brown dog and very timid. When Sakurako took Latte into Hinata's parents' veterinary clinic, the dog always barked at everyone.

"I—I will. Bye," he said, giving a quick bow and swiftly turning to leave.

"Tee-hee-hee. You're such a shy boy, Hinata," the elderly woman called out after him.

Mayuka chimed in and said, "He really is. Sorry, Miss Sakurako."

Who are you, my mom? Hinata grumbled inwardly. *Fine, say whatever you want. It's true that I'm not good at making conversation.*

"Hey, Hinata! Wait up!" Mayuka rushed after him.

He muttered under his breath, "And when…be able…?"

"Huh? What was that? Did you say something?" she asked, leaning in close.

Hinata bumped her with his shoulder to push her away. "I said, 'And when will you actually be able to afford any jewelry?'"

"Oh, how rude! In that case, I wonder when *you'll* actually be a proper veterinarian!"

Hinata clutched the book to his chest and turned his head away in a huff. "I haven't even decided if I'm going to be a vet or not!"

"Really? Then what will happen to the Marron Veterinary Clinic?!" she cried.

Hinata ignored her and started running. His family ran the Marron Veterinary Clinic, a three-story building on the edge of the shopping district with white painted walls. There was a red awning over the entrance with a cute sign featuring a drawing of a chestnut. The name and illustration were his parents' idea, because *marron* was French for "chestnut," which was also the meaning of the first kanji in their name, *Kuri*-hara.

He walked past the clinic's door and started climbing the stairs around the outside of the building. The entrance to the house was on the second floor. Hinata unlocked the door and walked through. Once he'd closed it, he leaned against the other side without taking off his backpack. He'd been running with the heavy book in his hands and was feeling out of breath.

"I wonder if Mayuka followed me."

He listened closely but didn't hear her feet coming up the steps. Maybe she'd gone home.

"No, she wouldn't. She'll be in the clinic."

Hinata set down the picture book, removed his pack, and turned around to go back toward the stairs.

Very carefully, Hinata pushed open the front door to the clinic. There was actually another door after the first one so that no animals in the waiting room could run outside when someone entered or left.

Once the automatic inner door opened, he saw a white-haired man sitting on the sofa in the lobby. Sure enough, Mayuka was already inside and talking with him.

"Really? This is a police dog?" she asked. "I thought they were supposed to be bigger!"

"You're right. Most of them are German shepherds or Labradors," said Hinata's grandfather, Shunya Oomori.

"Grandpa!" Hinata shouted with surprise and delight. "I didn't know you were coming today. Aren't you busy?"

Shunya beamed at his grandson and waved. "There you

are, Hinata. Well, you see, something came up all of a sudden. In fact, I wanted to ask you to do something for me."

Shunya was the father of Hinata's mother, Suzune. He lived by himself in a distant neighborhood near the river. But he wasn't lonely—he had dogs to keep him company.

While Shunya had been working his regular office job, he had studied to be a dog trainer on the side. And when Hinata's grandmother passed away and Shunya reached retirement age, he left the company and started a new job as a trainer. Now he raised dogs for the police and assisted with their investigations. Hinata loved his grandfather and had great respect for him.

"You need something from *me*?" Hinata asked.

"That's right. It's about this dog here…"

Resting at Shunya's feet was a Shiba Inu with light-brown fur. The dog lifted his head a little as Shunya rubbed it, then rested his chin back on his front paws. The poor thing didn't seem too happy.

"Is that a new dog? Right now you've got three German shepherds, right, Grandpa?"

Shunya nodded. "That's right. But now I'm taking care of this one, too. It seems like he might be better off as an only dog. I was wondering if I could ask you to look after him…"

"What? Hinata's going to have a dog?" asked Mayuka suddenly, her eyes sparkling. Her family and Hinata's were

close, so she was familiar with Shunya and enjoyed hearing his stories about police dogs.

"Y-you want me to take care of him? But…"

Hinata's face fell. His parents had told him they would never keep pets, because it was important to always place the animals at the clinic first.

But Shunya just grinned and said, "Actually, I've already cleared it with Yuusuke and Suzune. I was just waiting for you to come home. Right?"

He winked at the front desk, where Hinata's father, Yuusuke, stood. At their family clinic, Hinata's mother, Suzune, was the doctor, while Yuusuke was the nurse. Yuusuke was also a qualified pet groomer and could provide help with everything from health management to haircuts.

When he'd been in college, Hinata's dad had played rugby, and he still had a firm physique, but his facial features and personality were very, very gentle. Except for right now. At the moment, he looked cross.

"Were you going to say anything, Hinata?"

Oh, right! Hinata had been so distracted by his grandfather and the Shiba Inu that he had forgotten to greet his dad.

"Sorry. I'm home," Hinata said, downcast.

Yuusuke grinned. "Good! Welcome back. Now, as for what Grandpa just said, we've already given our blessing."

"R-really? But I've asked so many times before, and you never allowed me to have a pet..."

Hinata couldn't believe it. Once his parents made up their minds, things were set in stone. Back when he was in pre-school, he had begged to keep a stray kitten he'd picked up. But despite his tears and sobs, they'd promptly found a foster family to take it.

"Well, the circumstances this time are different," Yuusuke said, shrugging.

Shunya nodded, then petted the dog on the head again. The Shiba Inu lifted his snout and whined softly.

"This little pup was a promising police dog and even got to participate in an investigation, but there was some... trouble."

"Is that really a police dog? It's a Shiba!"

"Oh, believe me, this is a true police dog. A fellow trainer named Kobayashi put a lot of work into this one. He might be a rare breed for the job, but the dog's talent is unquestionable."

Hinata stared at the Shiba Inu. He had very nice soft fur, a fluffy curled tail, and intelligent-looking features, but the way the little white patches above his eyes moved made the dog seem very concerned.

"He looks kind of lonely," Hinata murmured.

Shunya nodded. "Kobayashi had to let the dog go, for

reasons of his own. So I took him in, but he's been so lifeless ever since. Plus…"

"Plus?" Mayuka repeated, looking over the Shiba with concern.

"He's terrified of bugs. Whenever one comes close, he gets spooked. It's hard to even take him for a walk, much less perform an investigation. Apparently, he got stung on the nose by a bee."

"Aww, poor thing!" Mayuka cried, covering her own nose with her hands. Hinata shivered. He'd read in a book that dogs had very sensitive noses. It must have hurt so much to get stung there.

"The poor pup," said Hinata with great sympathy. "So is he still a police dog?"

"No, he had to be retired from the force," admitted Shunya. "I feel awful. I saw how hard Kobayashi worked to get this dog ready. He's still only two years old. But what's done is done. The least we can do is give the dog a good home."

"Can I pet him?" Hinata asked his grandfather.

"Of course!"

Hinata crouched down and softly stroked the dog's head. He squeezed his eyes shut and lifted his chin a little.

"What's his name?"

"Christie. Kobayashi loves mystery novels, you see. He

took the name from the great mystery writer Agatha Christie. I've been calling the dog Chris for short."

"Good dog, Chris…"

Hinata took Chris's cheeks in his hands and squeezed them. Chris shut his eyes and happily stretched out his neck, allowing Hinata to rub under his chin.

"Chris is so cute," Mayuka said, crouching to examine the Shiba. "You're going to keep him, right, Hinata?"

Hinata started to say yes but suddenly felt overcome with worry. Being around the clinic had made him very aware that having a pet wasn't a decision to take lightly. Things rarely went as you thought they would. It was a lot of work to take care of a pet, and once you took one in, you couldn't just give up and back out. If he was going to keep this dog, he would have to take responsibility for him.

Before Hinata could answer, the sliding door to the examination room opened. A boy came out with a large brown tabby cat, then turned and gave a very polite bow.

"Thank you very much, Doctor. Go on, Chachamaru—say thanks…"

He tried to point the cat's face toward the exam room, but the animal only looked annoyed. His face was flat, like it'd been smooshed by the palm of someone's hand.

Suzune's voice came out from the exam room. "You're welcome, Rui. This is the sort of thing that happens to cats all the time, so don't worry. Bye-bye, Chachamaru."

"Oh! Rui Takeuchi! I didn't know you were here," said Mayuka, bounding toward the boy and his cat. Rui was one of their classmates. He used Chachamaru's head to help straighten up his slipping glasses.

"When I got back from school, I saw that Chachamaru had thrown up his food, so I brought him here to the vet. Grandma was too busy to leave home; one of her apprentices was visiting."

Rui's grandmother was a tea ceremony master. Everyone in their class knew how much of a grandma's boy he was. Even the way he talked sounded *old*. But Rui didn't seem to mind.

"Oh, Hinata, you're here," said Suzune, poking her head out of the room. "Nice to see you, Mayuka." She was short and round-faced, with her hair cut into a bob.

"Dr. Suzune! Hinata can keep Chris, right?" Mayuka said immediately.

Suzune glanced down at Hinata, who was crouched next to the dog.

"Well, it goes against our ethics to keep a pet when we run a vet clinic…but the poor thing's in a tough situation, and we thought that having a dog might help Hinata get over his shyness."

Really? That's why you're okay with it now? Hinata thought, aghast.

Mayuka giggled. "I know, right? His shyness is on a whole other level."

"Now, now," Shunya scolded. "Suzune. Mayuka. You should be more understanding about a young boy's tender feelings. Hinata is a very kindhearted child. That's a *good* thing."

From behind the counter, Yuusuke spoke up in his son's defense. "Don't you remember when we chose the characters in his name? First 'sun,' for being bright and full of life, and then 'poem,' with the hope that he would grow up to be rich with emotion. That's very important. It's who Hinata is."

Shunya beamed at his grandson. "That's right! And it's why I wanted to give Chris to you."

"Grandpa…"

He really does know me, Hinata thought. *He only brought Chris because he thought I would be up to the challenge.*

Hinata stood up, smacked both cheeks with his hands, and said, "A-all right. I'll take care of Chris. I can do it!"

Mayuka cheered and excitedly pumped her fist into the air. Even Rui looked happy about the development.

"It's wonderful having a pet," he said. "I'm more of a cat person, but I don't have any problem with dog people."

Even Chachamaru meowed in apparent approval.

After Rui left with his cat, Shunya gave Hinata a full explanation of Chris's situation.

This was a dog who had been trained to firmly obey his owner. He was completely housebroken and would not bite or otherwise attack people. Chris was a very smart and well-behaved dog.

"However, changing owners and homes is very stressful for a dog. He's probably going to be nervous and wary at first. But once Chris understands that his new human is trustworthy, things will go very smoothly."

Hinata's grandfather had other dogs to take care of, so he couldn't sit around all day. He waved goodbye, saying he'd be back later.

"Aw, today's Tuesday, isn't it?" said Mayuka. "I have to go study English conversation. I was hoping to play with Chris some more. Oh well." She made her way to the door of the clinic with obvious reluctance.

Once everyone else had gone, Hinata got his father's help in taking all the necessary items for the dog to their home upstairs. There was an indoor pen, potty pads, food and water dishes, and dog food.

"We can worry about the other stuff later," Yuusuke said, winking. "Thankfully, we have lots of supplies here at the clinic. Also, you'll want this."

He presented Hinata with a book called *A Happy Home Life with Your New Dog!*

"It's about how to care for a dog. It has lots of illustrations, so it's perfect for all ages. Chris was a police dog, so he's already well trained. But *you're* still new to this, Hinata."

"Th-thanks…"

Hinata set up the pen in the living room and put Chris inside it, then sat nearby and read the book.

Different breeds of dogs tended to have different temperaments. Shiba Inu were quick learners, brave, and active. They were very faithful to their owners but equally cautious around other people. They were often extremely guarded and might show aggression toward new people or things…

After reading that far, Hinata got very nervous. His mind began to spin.

What if Chris never gets used to me? What if he thinks I'm not trustworthy? Maybe he won't get over his old owner, and he'll stay depressed forever...

For the dog's part, Chris wriggled under a rumpled blanket until only his face stuck out, his eyes glancing all around. Shunya had given Hinata the blanket—it had been Chris's favorite ever since he was a puppy.

Is this really a good idea? Will Chris be happy with me as his owner?

Hinata was starting to feel pessimistic.

Later that night, Yuusuke was relaxing at the kitchen table with a cup of coffee. He called out to Hinata, "How do you feel about your new partner?"

Hinata was sitting cross-legged in front of the pen, staring at Chris. "I'm feeling the weight of responsibility."

"Responsibility? I see. Well, it *is* a lot."

"Hinata's too serious for his own good," Suzune said, sitting across from Yuusuke with her laptop open.

"There's nothing wrong with being serious," Yuusuke argued. "It's a good thing that he understands how big a responsibility this is."

"It might not be bad, but it's not good to overthink things, either. Building a relationship takes time. He just needs to relax and let it happen."

Hinata glanced back at his parents for a moment, then returned his gaze to Chris, resting his chin on his knees.

"Hinata?" his mother said. She was now standing next to him, looking down at her son and the dog. "There's no way to change the bad experiences Chris had in the past. So let's focus on what we can do: giving Chris a better life now. Don't worry—this isn't a bad place. Chris has a nice new owner and a very cool and handsome groomer, too. And best of all, he'll have a capable and talented vet taking care of him."

"Stop tooting your own horn, Suzu!" her husband said, laughing as he walked over. "But your mother's right, Son. People keep dogs because it makes both them and the dog happy. You can't have one without the other. So let's *all* be happy!"

Oh, I get it now! Hinata felt like a weight had been lifted from his shoulders. *I'll be okay, because I have my family. We'll all be happy together!*

...At least, that's how it was supposed to be! Hinata thought bitterly the next morning. It was six o'clock, and his parents were both still dreaming...

Right before bedtime last night, Suzune had said, "It'd

be a good idea to get into the habit of taking Chris on a walk before you go to school. This is a new environment, so for tomorrow, just focus on getting him used to the routine. Good luck!"

I knew I was gonna have to do everything on my own!

Hinata greeted Chris at the dog pen in the living room. "Good morning, Chris. Do you want to go for a walk?"

Like the day before, Chris was curled up in the blanket. He looked up at Hinata and whined.

"You like walks, don't you? Wanna go…?"

He opened the gate of the pen and called the dog again, but Chris did not move. *Hmmm, let's see…*

Hinata tried to remember what Grandpa Shunya would do when he took his dogs out for a walk. It seemed like he didn't have to do anything, and the dogs just naturally reacted. But because he was a trainer, he often spoke to the dogs…

I can do that, Hinata decided, and he got to his feet.

"Chris, come!" he commanded.

Chris slowly got to his feet, shook himself, and walked out of the pen. Steadily, the dog plodded over to Hinata's left side, turned to face the same direction, and plopped down into a seated position.

Hinata felt his pulse race. *Wow! Chris actually listened to me!*

Belatedly, he realized he should reward his dog for doing

what he'd asked. Hinata petted Chris on the head and said sincerely, "Good dog, Chris. Good dog."

Chris looked up at Hinata, as though waiting for his next words. Hinata put a red leash on Chris's collar and announced, "All right, let's go for a walk!"

He started walking, and Chris followed along. At the front door, Hinata slipped into his shoes, went outside, and started down the stairs. Chris trotted along right beside him.

Hinata was feeling great now. This was a very good sign. The weather was nice, and it was a pleasant, cool morning in early summer. He squeezed the leash handle and was just about to head out into the still-empty market when he stopped short with a start.

"Oh!"

Whoops, I forgot my walk supplies!

Last night, he had arranged all the things he'd need for this morning's walk: poop bags, tissues, a water bottle to rinse off any pee, and a small bag with a handful of dog kibble. He'd put them all in a little shoulder bag while consulting his book, but he hadn't picked it up before walking out the door.

"Sorry, Chris. I gotta go and get the bag."

He turned around to head back inside. But at that very moment, a white butterfly fluttered across their path.

"Oh, a cabbage butterfly…"

The insect avoided Hinata's outstretched hand and flitted toward Chris instead. And then…

"*Yipe!*"

Chris shrieked and immediately began to run.

"Aaah!"

A strong tug on the leash almost caused Hinata to fall. If the loop at the end hadn't been around his wrist, Chris would have bolted off right through the shopping district.

But because the leash held firm, Chris was yanked sideways. The dog yelped again and kicked frantically with his feet.

"Chris, what's wrong?" Hinata cried. "Chris!" He tried to get the dog upright, but Chris hopped up on his own and began pawing at his nose, running around desperately in circles. Hinata was stunned.

"*He's terrified of bugs,*" Shunya had told him.

"Oh, right! Chris got stung on the nose by a bee. Even butterflies are no good, huh?"

Hinata jumped over to Chris, who was spinning around in circles, and scooped him up into his arms. He tried to calm the dog, whispering soothingly into his ear. "It's all right, Chris. Just calm down. The butterfly won't hurt you. You'll be fine. There, there…"

After a little while, Chris finally stopped struggling. Now he was just panting heavily.

"Thank goodness," Hinata said, letting go of the dog.

Chris promptly plopped onto his bottom. "I think that's enough walking for today."

Chris looked up at Hinata, white eyebrows pinching together like the dog was about to cry.

"C'mon, let's go. Back up the stairs," Hinata said, tugging lightly on the leash, but Chris did not move. "What's wrong, Chris? Get up."

He tried a stronger pull, but Chris wouldn't budge. It seemed like the dog might not move from that spot ever again in his life. Chris even had his front legs pushed forward to hold himself in place.

"Chris, come!" Hinata ordered, but the dog refused. Left

with no other choice, Hinata got behind Chris, reached down, got his hands under his sides, and lifted. His idea was to shift the dog forward to get him moving, but Chris was much heavier than he'd realized.

By the time he'd reached the base of the steps, Hinata had to lower Chris back to the ground. He wouldn't be able to get him up the stairs. Hinata was ashamed to admit it, but he was one of the weaker boys in his class.

"Please, Chris, just walk!" he pleaded. But no matter what he did, Chris stubbornly stayed in place.

At a loss, and on the verge of tears, Hinata sat down on the lowest step.

A little over a week later, Chris was slowly getting used to his new home.

The dog had learned the family's daily schedule so that when Hinata woke up in the morning, Chris was happily wagging his tail as his owner emerged from his room. When the family was relaxing in the living area, Chris was almost always next to Hinata on the sofa.

Starting with their second walk, Hinata had learned to be very mindful of any nearby insects. If he saw one, he would quickly cross to the other side of the road and move past it, or wait for it to go away. As long as Chris didn't see the bugs, he didn't panic and didn't plop down and refuse to move. Chris walked with good posture and always followed Hinata's commands. It was obvious the dog had been trained well.

Hinata, too, was careful to remember his walk supplies and got used to cleaning up after Chris.

Suzune often repeated the story of their first walk. "It must've been really awful, huh? I didn't see either of you when I got up, so I rushed outside and found you both hugging each other and crying," she'd say, laughing.

"I wasn't crying! I just didn't know what to do, because Chris wouldn't move!" Hinata would protest every time. Chris would then chime in with a bark.

"You're even starting to act like each other," Suzune would say with a satisfied smile.

Mayuka often accompanied them on their evening walks. She and Hinata always had the same conversation.

"Hey, can I hold the leash?"

"No. Not until Chris gets more used to me."

"You're no fun. How much longer will that take?"

"Umm… Two weeks, maybe?"

When people saw Hinata walking Chris, they would often call out to him. Without realizing it, he was having a lot more interactions with new people.

"Aww, what a cute Shiba. What's his name?"

"The breed is actually called Shiba Inu. And his name is Chris," Mayuka would say. She was always the one who responded while Hinata took a step back. Holding a light and bubbly conversation the way Mayuka did was still too much for him.

"Having a dog might help Hinata get over his shyness," his mom had said, but Hinata didn't think it would be that simple. Still, he couldn't help but smile whenever someone said Chris was cute.

One of the people who talked to them on their walks was a young patrol officer from the local police station.

When Mayuka explained to him that Chris was a former police dog, the officer had said, "Wow! A Shiba Inu police dog? That's impressive!"

He revealed that he had actually taken the job because he wanted to be a trainer for police dogs.

"But I ended up doing routine patrol duty," he said with chagrin. By now, Officer Iwata had already become a familiar face.

Another person they came to know was a college student who lived in a little apartment near the police station. The first time he spoke to them, both Hinata and Mayuka backed away with apprehension due to his appearance.

He was very tall, at nearly six feet, and his hair was bleached blond and spiked. He wore flashy T-shirts that looked like they'd been splattered with all kinds of paint and tattered vintage jeans. He even had a number of gold piercings in his ears and often wore sunglasses. But when he took his shades off and crouched down to get a good look at Chris, the college student's face broke into a sappy, slack-jawed grin, like he couldn't be happier.

"I love Shiba Inu. They're so cute," he said. "We used to have one back home, but it died when I was in the fourth grade… Man, I cried so much."

Hinata and Mayuka had exchanged surprised glances. They realized then that the saying was true: You couldn't judge a book by its cover.

"Do you mind if I give your pup another pat next time? My name's Takaki

Moriyama, and I'm a college student. I live in this apartment building."

"I'm Mayuka, this is Hinata, and the dog's name is Chris," Mayuka told him.

Takaki smiled at them kindly and said, "Then you're 'Chris and Friends' to me! See ya later!"

Ever since, Takaki's apartment had been part of their route.

One day, Hinata stumbled across a book he'd left on his desk and forgotten about. It was the photo book of animals he'd borrowed from the school library on the day he met Chris. The return due date was approaching, but he hadn't even opened it yet.

Hinata flipped through the pages and was surprised that he wasn't as fascinated with the pictures as before. When he'd first found it, he had been thinking that becoming a nature photographer would be much more interesting than being a veterinarian.

It's weird that what I want to be changes so much. Now I find myself thinking it would be nice to be a dog trainer. I guess it's because all I can think about is Chris...

When he admitted this to Suzune, she laughed and said, "You're only in elementary school. Of course you can't decide on just one dream yet. As you grow up, you'll keep finding new dreams to think about. That's just how life is."

The Jewel Thief and
the Little Lost and Found

It was the second Sunday since Chris had arrived.

"Come, Chris. It's time for your walk!"

It was early morning as Hinata headed out into the empty shopping district as always, stretching his muscles. It was past mid-May, and the sunlight was getting stronger every day, but this early it was still cool and crisp.

"Which way should we go today?"

Chris looked to the right, so Hinata started walking away from the train station, toward the police station. It was the weekend, and the shopping district was still asleep, except for the sound of light footsteps coming toward them. They belonged to a young man who jogged right past Hinata and Chris.

Chris turned and whined softly as the man ran by. This was something Hinata had noticed from their walks together. When Chris saw a young man, the dog tended to look sad and whine. He was probably thinking of Mr. Kobayashi, his former owner.

One of the passages in *A Happy Home Life with Your New Dog!* had said that Shiba Inu were "*very faithful to their owners but equally cautious around other people.*" That made Hinata feel kind of bad. *I thought we were getting along well, but I guess I can't replace Chris's old owner…*

He sighed and started walking again, when a bicycle came whizzing past from a side street.

It's gonna hit us! Hinata thought, and he tumbled into the street to protect Chris.

Screeee!

The bike just barely managed to avoid hitting the two of them.

"Hey, watch where you're going!" the bicyclist yelled before continuing on his way.

"Owww," Hinata groaned, sitting up. "Are you all right, Chris?"

Chris had been startled by the sudden event, too, and was hopping in place with his ears flat against his head. The dog hadn't been struck by the bike, at least.

Hinata was relieved but felt like he wanted to cry. *That guy was a real jerk! Yeah, it's my fault for not paying attention, but he shouldn't be riding that fast. And he didn't have to yell…*

As he got to his feet, feeling disgruntled, he caught a

glimpse of his knee, and he fell into the road again. "Ah! It's b-bleeding…"

Hinata was not very tough when it came to injuries. The sight of even a little bit of blood would make him light-headed. Without letting go of the leash, he pressed his hand around his knee and clenched his eyes shut. *Owww…*

"Whine, whine…"

Chris's breath was warm on Hinata's face. The dog barked a few times and poked Hinata on the cheek. But Hinata couldn't get up or even open his eyes.

Suddenly, the leash slipped right out of his hands.

"Huh? Chris?" Hinata said, lifting his head. As he did, he saw Chris dashing off as fast as his legs would carry him. The red leash, bright in the morning sun, bounced along the road's surface.

"Chris!"

Oh no! Hinata tried to get up, but he lost his balance and landed on his bottom again. On the third try, he finally got to his feet. He trained his eyes in the direction Chris had gone. There was no sign of the dog anywhere.

"Chris! Chris, where are you?!" Hinata shouted, growing pale. *What should I do? Chris has gotten lost!*

He dragged his wounded leg behind him, on the verge of tears. If anything happened to Chris, it would be his own fault as the dog's owner. *How could I let Chris go, just because I got a scrape?!*

From somewhere in the empty shopping area came the barking of a dog. It was frantic and constant. Hinata then heard a high-pitched female voice speaking back.

"What is it? What's going on, Chris? Did you take yourself for a walk this time?"

As Hinata stumbled in the direction of the voice, Chris's head popped out from an alley a short distance away. When the dog saw Hinata, his ears popped upright, and he came racing over.

"Chris!"

Hinata held out his arms, and Chris launched into them. Hinata was bowled over backward, and he fell onto his bottom yet again. The dog was on top of him now, licking his face over and over. Hinata giggled and laughed, hugging his partner.

"Thank goodness, Chris! I thought you got lost…"

"Oh! Hinata? What's the matter? Are you all right?"

Hinata looked up with a start and saw a girl gazing down at him with concern, a white toy poodle in her arms.

"Oh, Yukina…"

Yukina was one of the Marron Clinic's regulars. She was a lively girl in her first year of middle school who loved to sing.

"I was taking Linda for a walk when Chris came speeding over to us, barking. I was so startled… Uh-oh, you skinned your knee!"

Yukina set Linda down and got some bandages out of her shoulder bag, which she promptly used to cover up Hinata's scrapes. They had cute cherry patterns on them. It was a little embarrassing, but Hinata was more relieved that his knee was taken care of.

"Th-thanks…"

She giggled and said he was welcome, then petted Chris on the head. "So you came to get help because your owner was hurt? Good dog, Chris!"

"Huh?"

"That's right. He was barking and barking, trying to get my attention. What a smart doggy!"

Oh, Chris was trying to help me… Hinata felt his chest grow hot. He hugged Chris again. *Thank you, Chris.*

Sorry for being a weak owner and getting hurt from such a little fall."

Hinata scooped up Chris's red leash, got to his feet, and looked his dog in the eyes. Chris wagged his fluffy tail, as though saying he was glad Hinata was all right.

"Well, we should start back home. I'm starving," said Yukina. In the distance they could hear the sound of a police car siren. "Hmm? What could be going on this early in the morning?"

She shaded her eyes with a hand, looking toward the station. Hinata did the same thing—the sun was bright this morning.

The siren was getting closer. Eventually, once the sound was so loud it almost hurt, a police car appeared and stopped near the station. Its lights bounced off the buildings in the area, even brighter than the sun. They could hear the car doors opening and slamming.

Linda barked with fright, and Yukina scooped her up. "There, there, it's all right. What could be going on? Did something happen at the station?"

Chris wasn't frightened, though. Maybe his time as a police dog had gotten him used to the sound of sirens.

Speaking of which, the four of them could hear another

siren in the distance, and this time it wasn't alone. Now there
was an ambulance, too. Soon the entire shopping district was
full of wailing sirens. People started poking their heads out
of doors and exclaiming over the fuss.

"Oh no! I'll go check it out!" Yukina said, rushing off
toward the station with Linda in her arms.

Hinata's heart was racing, and he could feel his knees
shaking. "M-maybe we should go home, Chris…"

But Chris looked back at Hinata and barked once, as if
to say, "Something's afoot! Shouldn't we go see?"

Hinata swallowed and glanced at the police cars again.

*Wait a second… Isn't that Sakura Jewelry they're in front
of? Is Miss Sakurako all right? And what about Latte the Chihuahua? The poor little thing's always terrified and barking…*

"A-all right, we'll go see, but just for a moment," he murmured, gripping the leash. Maybe with Chris they'd be fine.

By the time they started running down the street, Hinata
had forgotten all about the pain in his knee.

The scene outside Sakura Jewelry was quite chaotic.

There were three police cars, an ambulance, and even a
so-called unmarked car with police lights on top, all parked
out front. Police officers were hurrying in and out of the jewelry store and trying to maintain order among the people
who had come to watch.

Hinata was stunned. How could something like this

happen right in his own neighborhood? What could be the matter?

Yukina was already there, stretching up on her tiptoes to see over the crowd. Hinata walked up to her and tapped her on the back.

"Oh! Hinata," she said, spinning around, her eyes sparkling with curiosity. "There was a break-in at Sakura Jewelry. Someone said the glass was broken."

A break-in?! A shiver ran down Hinata's spine at the thought. Chris barked.

"Oh, Chris! If only you'd been there to help. Latte isn't much of a guard dog—not that Linda would be, either. There's only so much a Chihuahua can do," Yukina said with a sigh.

Hinata fretted. "…Is everything okay?"

"I'm not sure. I wonder how Miss Sakurako's doing. There's an ambulance here, after all…"

She rose up on her tiptoes again to look at the vehicle. Hinata tried to lean around the person in front of him to see.

"Waaah!"

Hinata yelped as someone clapped him on the shoulder from behind. He spun around and saw that it was Yuusuke.

"Dad!"

"Take Chris back home right now, Hinata. It's dangerous

here, and you shouldn't be getting in the way of a police investigation."

Suzune was behind him. They both had jackets on, but it was clear they'd simply tossed them over their indoor clothes and rushed outside.

"B-but Miss Sakurako and Latte…"

"Yes, I know. Let the police take care of Miss Sakurako. We'll ask about Latte," said Suzune. She slipped through the bystanders and spoke to an officer handling the crowd. "Excuse me, I'm a veterinarian just down the street…"

Yuusuke patted Hinata on the shoulder again. "Go on—wait for us back home. We'll let you know what we find out."

Hinata obeyed, pulling Chris's leash in the direction of home. The whole thing was starting to scare him, so he was glad his parents had come.

But Chris seemed curious about the scene and kept turning around to look as they walked away.

"I hear a helicopter. I bet they're filming an aerial shot for the news," Yuusuke murmured, sitting cross-legged on the floor of the living room. Latte shivered between his legs. "The media were there reporting on the incident. Oh, I hope Miss Sakurako's all right…"

The owner of Sakura Jewelry had been taken to the hospital in an ambulance, so for the moment, Hinata's parents had decided to keep Latte at the clinic. Because Latte hated the doctor, it was Yuusuke's job to watch over the Chihuahua.

Suzune examined Latte's medical file on the computer. "She was quite shocked about the robbery. And she's not young anymore, of course. It's better for someone to be watching over her in the hospital right now. I think Latte's fine, aside from the fright. There's no record of any major illnesses in here…"

"I wonder if the shop was badly damaged during the break-in."

"Well, we can't exactly ask Miss Sakurako, can we? I doubt we'll know how much was lost until her son can confirm it. It might be a small shop, but they do sell jewelry. It's not like stealing apples from the supermarket."

"I know," Yuusuke said. "I've heard of jewel heists, but I've never heard of an apple heist."

While his parents didn't seem all that concerned, Hinata was balled up on the couch, hugging his knees. "Yukina said the glass window was broken."

Even Chris seemed to be listening in. The dog's ears twitched every now and then.

"Yes," Suzune replied. "It happened late at night, before dawn. Sakurako noticed it when she got up in the morning. They'd even deactivated her security system. Seems like the work of professionals."

"Professionals? At what?"

"Stealing. There's a group of thieves that have been swiping jewelry all over the place."

Hinata's eyes went wide, and he stared at Chris, who looked back at him with concern.

"Is *our* home safe…?" he murmured. His bandaged knee felt like it was going to start hurting again.

"We don't have any jewelry here," Suzune said with a laugh. "And if they're smart, they won't keep targeting the same area. The police are on the hunt for them now."

That made Hinata feel a little better, at least.

After lunch, Hinata took Chris back outside. They had barely done any walking in the morning, and he felt bad about it, but mostly he was concerned about the day's big event. There were still police cars and officers near the station. Suzune said it was safe now, but he wasn't brave enough to wander closer to the scene of the crime.

"Let's go that way, Chris," he said, walking in the other direction, when all of a sudden a person came running their way, waving.

"Hinata!"

It was Mayuka. She ran up to him, breathing heavily.

"H-hey, did you see the midday news?"

"No. What happened?"

"You didn't hear?! Sakura Jewelry was broken into! It's a big case. It was even on TV! How could you not know?"

Hinata jabbed his thumb over his shoulder at the cars behind them. "I saw it all this morning. The police are still over there…"

"Well, stop playing dumb, then! What about Miss Sakurako? Is she all right?"

"She got taken to the hospital…"

"What? Did the thief attack her?!"

"N-no. I think she was just in shock."

"How terrible…," Mayuka said, wiping a tear from the corner of her eye and sniffling. "It must be so scary to be robbed. And she lives alone, too. I bet it was really upsetting."

"…That's really sweet of you to say, Mayuka," said Hinata, taken aback by his usually peppy friend's sudden display of tenderness.

"When I get older, I want to be like her. My grandma isn't as cool as Miss Sakurako! She's just an old lady."

I take back everything nice I just said! Your grandma's a great person who really cares about you! And here I was, thinking you were being kind…

Mayuka rubbed her eyes again and murmured, "I'll go and visit her once she's out of the hospital."

Sheesh, Hinata thought. *But I guess she really is worried about Miss Sakurako.*

"Do you think they've caught the culprit? Should we go ask those officers over there?" she suggested.

Hinata's eyes bugged out. "What?! I—I don't think that's a good idea… They're still busy examining the crime scene. They're going to yell at us for getting in their way."

"Maybe… But aren't you curious about the case?"

"W-well, sure, I am, but… Oh, I know! Why don't we ask Officer Iwata at the local station?" Hinata said. "That's probably better than hanging around the crime scene. And we know him, right?" He was very relieved when Mayuka pumped her fist triumphantly.

"You're so smart, Hinata. Let's do that! Officer Iwata patrols this area. He'll know what's going on."

They ran off in the opposite direction toward the police station, with Chris in tow. Beyond the shopping district was a large street. The station was just on the other side.

"Officer Iwaaata!" Mayuka cried, rushing up to the man standing in front of the station.

His expression, normally diligent and attentive, softened into a kind smile when he saw them. "Well, if it isn't Mayuka and Hinata! You're here early today. Oh, but it's Sunday, isn't it?"

"Hey, about the break-in at the jeweler's this morning! Did they catch the thief?" Mayuka asked.

Immediately, the officer grimaced. "I closed up the

station this morning to assist at the scene but came back here in the afternoon. There's been no progress so far. It might take a while… But I'm sure you're nervous, since it happened so close to home."

"Yeah! And we know the owner, Miss Sakurako, really well. She's our friend."

"Ahh… We were even on alert because there was a bag snatcher in the next neighborhood over two days ago," said Iwata. "I'm pretty frustrated that we let something like this happen anyway."

He crouched down and pet Chris on the head.

"Your buddies might be hard at work on the scene as we speak, Chris. That excellent canine sense of smell can be very helpful in cases like this one."

Chris wagged his tail proudly, as if to say, "You bet it can." At that, Mayuka turned to Hinata and said, "That's it! Hinata, why don't we take Chris to go help the police? Chris is really smart, so I'm sure we'll catch the—"

"N-no!" Hinata stammered, holding up his hand. "Chris retired from the force."

Iwata also tried to talk her down. "That's right! And even active police dogs can't just be milling around a crime scene without an expert trainer handling them. The dogs and officers on the scene are doing their best already…"

Mayuka puffed out her cheeks, sulking. "But it would be

so cool if Chris solved the crime… And I bet Miss Sakurako would be happy about it, too."

"That's not the point," Hinata protested, irritated at Mayuka's refusal to listen. He tugged on Chris's leash. "I'm going to continue our walk…"

He bowed politely to Officer Iwata and started off. The policeman grimaced and said, "Be careful, Hinata. And, Mayuka, you'd better stay away from that crime scene!"

"Boo! Both of you, always telling me no, no, no!"

"Of course we are!" Hinata snapped as he walked away. "This is a real investigation we're talking about. It's not something from a comic book or a movie. Kids aren't supposed to go around poking their noses into police investigations." Hinata was normally so reserved that his unexpected outburst really got to Mayuka. In the end, she followed along without further comment.

Eventually, Hinata passed through the torii gate of the Tenso Shrine. This was one of his and Chris's usual walk routes. Once inside the Shinto shrine's grounds, leafy branches and bushes blocked out much of the sunlight, making it much darker than outside.

Mayuka still said nothing. She was normally so talkative

that Hinata was a little surprised. He glanced down at Chris as they walked along the stone path to the shrine.

The next moment, Chris came to a stop and stared at a patch of ground next to the path.

"Huh?" Hinata trained his eyes on the spot and saw something small and black lying there. "What is it, Chris?"

He crouched down to get a better look. Chris lowered his snout to sniff at the object, and Mayuka peered over Hinata's shoulder.

"Oh, an earphone."

She's right. It was an earbud, the kind of wireless earphone that went all the way into your ear, used for communication or for listening to music…

"Those are supposed to be really expensive. One of my older cousins was bragging about his," Mayuka said. She reached out for the earbud, but Hinata stopped her.

"H-hang on a moment."

He stared at Chris. When that bicyclist had nearly hit him this morning, Chris had done his best to help him. Hinata felt he needed to be an even better owner to Chris in return. Maybe now, his thoughts would reach Chris's mind somehow.

Chris was staring back at Hinata. The dog's eyes sparkled.

Let's go! he thought.

Hinata opened the shoulder bag with all his walk supplies

inside and pulled out a plastic bag. He stuck it over his right hand and picked up the earbud so that he wasn't touching it directly. Then he held it up to Chris's nose. What was it that his grandfather would say to his dogs, again?

"Chris, smell!"

The dog sniffed at the earbud. Mayuka's face lit up, and she asked, "Oh… Are you going to have Chris search for the owner?"

Uncertainly, Hinata replied, "W-well…I don't know if this will work, but I think it's worth a try. Earbuds go inside the ear, so they should smell a lot like the owner. I watched Grandpa train his dogs, so I think I know how to do it. We can't catch the jewel thief, but maybe we can do something…"

"Let's try it! I'm sure we'll find something! Wow, this is so exciting!" Mayuka exclaimed. She was getting a bit carried away.

"Shhh, quiet," Hinata cautioned. "Let Chris focus on the smell in peace."

Mayuka clamped her mouth shut and watched Chris work. The dog sniffed and sniffed, then looked at Hinata. He seemed to be waiting for a command.

Hinata folded up the earbud in the plastic bag and stood. He was ready to give the next order.

"Now *search*!"

Chris immediately marched off, holding his nose right next to the ground, traveling straight down the path leading to the shrine itself. He passed between the pair of lion-dog statues, up two stone steps, and toward the entrance of the shrine.

"Th-this is amazing," Mayuka whispered, marveling. "Chris is really following the scent. I guess the earbud's owner must have come here to pray."

Chris sniffed around the offering box, then lifted his nose and started to circle the shrine. Hinata quickly tugged on the leash. "W-wait, Chris! You can't go that way…"

He had seen a number of insects that looked like bees flying around between the roof of the shrine and some hanging branches leaning over it. The last thing he wanted was for Chris to fly into a panic.

This time, Chris returned to the spot where they'd found the earbud, then continued onward, back to the torii gate.

"Did the owner pray, then go home?" Mayuka wondered. That seemed likely to Hinata. Whatever the case, Chris appeared to know the route the owner had taken. The dog began to pull even harder on the leash.

Chris passed through the gate and immediately turned left. "Toward the police station," Mayuka murmured. As he walked along the sidewalk in front of the station, Chris was bobbing his head in the breeze, still following the scent. Then the dog came to a stop and sat down in front of the crosswalk beyond.

"Wow, Chris can tell when there's a red light," Mayuka murmured, amazed. Hinata felt the same way. Chris's ability to track a scent was impressive enough, but to be able to recognize details about the environment and react accordingly was remarkable.

When the light turned green and the cars stopped, Chris pressed his nose against the ground and began to stride across the street.

"Toward the shopping district," Mayuka noted. Indeed, the trail was taking Chris precisely in that direction. They entered the neighborhood, passed the Marron Veterinary Clinic, and then…

"Hinata, do you think—?"

Mayuka was right: The scent was leading right to the scene of the heist at Sakura Jewelry. Chris came to a stop right in front of the yellow police tape they had put up around the building. There was still a single patrol car parked in front of the jewelry store.

Uh-oh, we're back here, Hinata thought, sighing heavily.

Sakurako's son was out front, speaking with a police officer. Next to him was a tall, fashionably dressed woman. She was very attractive and looked to be in her midthirties.

They could hear the son addressing the officer, saying "This is the president of the company I work for."

Hinata and Mayuka were standing there, listening in, when a uniformed officer said to them, "You kids aren't allowed to be here. Go on—move back."

"Okay, but—" Mayuka tried to explain. Hinata, however, grabbed her arm and whispered, "F-forget it, Mayuka. The scent might have already disappeared up ahead. And there are too many people to get past."

"But...but...," she protested.

He pulled her arm again. "Come on, let's give up. We'll hand the earbud over to Officer Iwata. It was a lost item in the first place, so we're supposed to turn it in to the lost and found at the station."

Mayuka realized he was right and started to turn around in the direction of the station—right as Chris began to pull at the leash, his nose pointed at the ground once again.

"You want to go to the station, too, Chris?" Mayuka asked. But Hinata realized Chris was now on a different scent trail. There was an insistence to the way the Shiba was tugging on the leash.

They passed the vet clinic once again as they left the shopping area. After crossing at the traffic light, they assumed Chris would return to the shrine, but instead, the dog turned the other way. Chris was indeed following a different trail. Perhaps the owner of the earbud had been walking all over.

When they passed by the station, Officer Iwata was looking at a work computer at a desk in the back. They continued, and a little while later, Chris turned down a narrow street to the right. They were now in a quiet residential area. The dog proceeded straight until he reached a gap in a concrete block wall to the left and stopped. This was the entry to an older two-story apartment building.

"This is where that punk rocker Takaki lives!" Mayuka shouted. Hinata recalled the man's flashy appearance.

"Come on, Mayuka. You should still call him 'mister.' He's a lot older than us."

"Yeah, I know he's a college student, but he seems so childish. It feels weird to get all formal with him."

Chris entered the apartment lot, walked to the door of the rightmost unit on the ground floor, and sat down. Then he barked once.

"Wow, what a coincidence! That's Takaki's—…" Just then, Mayuka was interrupted by a loud voice from inside. Hinata pulled back a bit on Chris's leash as the door slammed open.

"Well, forget you! Clearly, you can't be bothered to care about me, either!" yelled the young woman who stormed out. She wore a bright-pink jacket and the same kind of torn-up jeans that Takaki did. Her bleached brown hair was feathered and gathered at the side of her head with a colorful tie.

"Oh!" she exclaimed, stopping when she saw the kids. "Who are you?"

"Wait up, Rinka! I *do* care about you. I just…"

Takaki popped his head out of the doorway and froze, just as the young woman had. "Oh! It's Chris and Friends. Chris, Hinata, and Mayuka. My little pals!"

He jumped out into the open, reached down to hug Chris, and rubbed his cheek against the dog's fur. Chris seemed slightly annoyed by this but allowed it with a show of impeccable politeness.

"Your 'pals'? A dog and some little kids? I guess that suits you," Rinka said snidely. Hinata and Mayuka looked a bit offended, but she kept talking to them anyway. "Listen to this! Don't you think Takaki's weird? If someone steals your bag, you'd tell the police about it, right?"

"A bag was stolen?" Mayuka repeated, stunned by the woman's statement.

This all sounded somehow familiar to Hinata, like he'd just heard about something similar. In fact, it reminded him of what Officer Iwata had said—that the police were on the lookout because of a theft two days ago.

"That's right," Rinka said. "His bag was stolen right outside the station this morning. You'd go to the police, right?"

"It's fine!" Takaki insisted, still petting Chris. "There wasn't anything worthwhile in there. My phone and wallet were in my pockets."

But Rinka was having none of it. She used the palm of her hand to flatten Takaki's spiky hair. "It's not fine at all! I bought you that shoulder bag as a birthday present! It was one half of a matching pair that I got for us just last month."

She slipped a black cloth bag off her shoulder. The golden fastener had a star-shaped charm dangling from it.

"It makes no sense not to inform the police when something important to you is stolen. Or are you saying my present wasn't important to you? That's how you really feel, isn't it?"

"I keep telling you, you've got it all wrong! I care about you, Rinka, and I care about the bag, too, but it's not a big enough deal to bother the cops about. They're busy, too, you know."

All Hinata and Mayuka could do was watch them fight in stunned silence.

"Forget it—I'm leaving!" Rinka shouted. "I suppose you've forgotten my birthday, too. It's only *next week*!" Then she

turned away in a huff and ran out through the gap in
the concrete block wall.

Takaki sighed heavily and muttered to Chris, "I didn't forget. And I want to get her a nice present, but I need money
for that...don't I, Chris?"

Chris just tilted his head in confusion.

"Are you sure you shouldn't tell the police about the theft?"
asked Mayuka.

Takaki got to his feet and looked up at the sky. Hesitantly,
Hinata added, "I—I agree..."

"You should report it," Mayuka said again. "We asked at

the police station earlier, and the officer said there was a theft in a nearby neighborhood recently!"

Takaki looked at her, surprised. "The police station?"

"Yeah. We're friends with the officer there."

Takiaki murmured, his eyes wide with amazement. "That's really something. Friends with a cop."

Suddenly, Mayuka shouted, "Oh yeah, Hinata! Remember what we're here for…"

He'd completely forgotten. Hinata took out the plastic bag. "…We found this…"

As soon as Takaki saw what was inside, he bolted upright and lunged over. "What? Wh-where? Where'd you find it? That's mine!"

So it was true. Hinata handed the plastic bag to Takaki as Mayuka proudly explained, "It was on the ground at Tenso Shrine. Chris followed the scent trail all the way here."

"At the shrine, huh…?" Takaki repeated, his eyes wandering a little. Then he seemed to finish processing what he'd heard. "Wait, you said Chris followed the trail?"

"Chris is a former police dog. Chris can figure out *anything*," Mayuka bragged, her hands on her hips and her chin boldly jutting forward.

Takaki's mouth hung open. "P-police dog…?"

"Yeah. Cool, right?"

He shook the plastic bag and muttered, "I had no idea… Chris, a police dog…" He glanced back and forth between Hinata and Mayuka. "I bought these earbuds and paid my rent, and I had no money left… And then, to top it all off, I lost one of them. Let me tell you, it really sucked. Thanks, guys. You've been a big help." He bowed and then said apologetically, "I've got to go to work soon, so I'll have to show you my appreciation some other time…"

"It's okay. You don't have to give us anything. You just said you don't have any money. Right, Hinata?" said Mayuka. He nodded.

Takaki smiled sheepishly. "Maybe I'll buy Chris some jerky, then. I should be getting paid pretty soon."

He waved, then abruptly shut the door, leaving Hinata and Mayuka standing outside his apartment.

"That was weird," Mayuka said. "Takaki was being really vague about everything."

Hinata shared a look with Chris and murmured, "He said he got robbed this morning near the station… But the jewelry store heist happened right nearby, so there would've been cop cars and officers all over. Would someone really try to steal a bag in a place like that? And in that case, why would Mr. Takaki take a detour to the shrine, rather than going straight home…?"

Mayuka snorted. "Maybe he was praying that his bag would come back."

Hinata wasn't so sure. He tugged at Chris's red leash. "C'mon, Chris, let's go home. Good job today. You were amazing."

Mayuka clapped her hands together, leaned over, and rubbed the dog on the head. "That's right! You were so smart. You're the best, Chris!"

Chris's tongue lolled, and he barked happily.

Mysteries Abound

On the way home from school the next day, Hinata and Mayuka made their way through the shopping district. The police tape had been removed from Sakura Jewelry, so they could walk past it. But the store itself was shuttered up, and there was a sign out front that said TEMPORARILY CLOSED.

"It's so sad to see the shutters down," Mayuka murmured, frowning.

"Yeah," Hinata agreed.

"I wonder how Miss Sakurako's doing…"

"They said she was shocked, but she wasn't hurt. Her son came over yesterday and filled us in. She should be out of the hospital tomorrow."

"Oh, I'm so glad!" Mayuka exclaimed, clasping her hands anxiously. "I hope she'll be able to reopen soon."

Hinata only sighed. Mayuka noticed this and pouted.

"Aren't you happy about Miss Sakurako getting out of the hospital, Hinata?"

"It's not that simple, unfortunately," he said, shaking his head. He remembered her son's grave tone the night before.

It would be difficult to reopen the jewelry store. The damage was serious—not only would the broken windows and cases need to be replaced, but so would the shop's stock of jewelry. And was it really all right for Sakurako to run the shop on her own after this?

Hinata had been listening in from a distance, but he could tell how big a deal it was. It was upsetting just to hear.

His parents hadn't been able to find the words to make everything better. The best they could do was to tell the man not to worry about Latte and to urge him to stop by again once Sakurako was out of the hospital.

Hinata's knowing expression irritated Mayuka. "Are you saying I don't understand because I'm just a kid? You're a kid, too, you know!"

She turned away in a huff, pigtails bouncing, and ran off.

It's true she didn't hear all the things I heard, so of course she wouldn't understand, Hinata thought, scratching his head. He started to hurry after Mayuka, just as someone exited the clinic and nearly collided with her.

"Oh, I'm so sorry!" she apologized immediately.

"Grandpa!"

It was Shunya. Hinata rushed over, and the elderly man put an arm around both of their shoulders and hugged them.

"I'm glad to see you kids are so full of energy," he said with a laugh. "Just don't forget that sometimes we old folks have to use the sidewalk, too."

"You're not old, Grandpa!" Hinata protested.

"Really? Then why are you calling me 'Grandpa'?" he replied, putting on a fake frown. Hinata and Mayuka laughed loudly.

"How about this?" Mayuka suggested. "'You might be old, but you act like a child!'"

Shunya made a funny face and said, "That feels even less like a compliment… Anyway, Hinata, I'm here to see Chris. Is he upstairs?"

"Yeah. The clinic gets crowded around this time of day, so Chris is watching the house."

"I asked Yuusuke, and he said things were going well. Are you two good friends now?"

"Yeah, we're best buds. Now hurry, Grandpa!"

Hinata pulled on Shunya's hand. The three of them went up the stairs, unlocked the door, and made their way inside.

"Chris!"

The moment the three of them stepped into the living room, Chris came bounding up. When the dog noticed Shunya, he wagged his fluffy tail and barked loudly.

"Good dog, Chris. Why, look how energetic you are now. Looks like you've settled in here, haven't you?" Shunya said, petting the dog, whose eyes narrowed with pleasure. But after sniffing at Shunya's clothes a bit, Chris whined sadly. Hinata wasn't sure how to feel about that.

"I wonder if seeing you again made Chris remember his old owner…"

Shunya patted his grandson on the shoulder. "Don't worry about that, Hinata. Chris's best friend right now is you."

"That's right, Hinata," Mayuka said, tossing her backpack on the floor. "I wish you could have seen Chris yesterday, Mr. Shunya. It was incredible!"

"Oh? And what did Chris do? Why don't we have an afternoon snack while you tell me all about it," Shunya suggested, beaming and holding up the cake box in his hand.

Mayuka cheered, "Yay, cake! We have so much to tell you about. Right, Hinata?"

"Yeah, there was a huge incident in the shopping area… Did Dad tell you about the jewelry heist?"

They each got something to drink and sat at the kitchen table, enjoying the cake slices Shunya had brought. Hinata and Mayuka took turns relating the twists of the jewelry store break-in and how Chris had tracked down the owner of the missing earbud.

Twirling her fork, Mayuka finished, "And then Chris

walked right up to Takaki's apartment door and barked. And it turned out Takaki really was the owner of the earbud!"

Shunya nodded. "I see. So he went from the station to the shrine, dropped his earbud there, then walked back home. And Chris followed the scent trail the whole way. That's very impressive."

Excitedly, Hinata added, "And Chris can tell when the traffic light is red. I didn't have to say anything; Chris just waited for it to turn green."

"Very good. Chris has been through a lot of training, after all."

"It seems like such a waste for Chris to quit being a police dog," Mayuka said. "Can't he join the force again?"

Hinata's grandfather shook his head. "That would be very difficult. For one thing, he can't stand bugs."

"What if you used bug spray?" suggested Mayuka. "I use it when I play outside in the summer. Is it bad for dogs or something?"

"There's bug spray for dogs, too," Hinata explained. "I had Dad try it out a few days ago. But Chris has a really sensitive nose and doesn't like the stuff. The spray was making him sneeze."

"Well then, couldn't he just avoid any bugs? Hinata's been doing a good job of leading Chris around the insects on their walks."

Shunya shook his head. "You can't choose where to go when you're conducting an investigation, Mayuka."

But Mayuka wasn't satisfied. Hinata, however, understood what Shunya was saying. He remembered their very first walk, when Chris had been spooked by a tiny butterfly. No police dog could do a proper job if something like that happened during an investigation.

"There's something else, too," said Shunya. "During Chris's first investigation as a professional police dog, there was a major problem."

"A problem?" Hinata asked, leaning forward. He had always been curious as to why Chris had to leave his former owner. Could the problem Shunya had mentioned have something to do with it?

"The case Chris was working on turned out to be much bigger and more difficult than anyone realized at first. It hasn't been solved yet, and the police still don't know who was responsible. Unfortunately, Chris had to separate from his trainer, Kobayashi, during the investigation," Shunya explained, his expression grave. "What's concerning is that Chris might have seen something the investigators aren't aware of. Chris can't tell us anything, of course, so we have no way of knowing what that might be. But the culprits might think Chris is a liability and try to hurt him…"

Hinata swallowed. This was turning out to be a much scarier story than he had realized.

"That's why we decided to remove Chris from the police program. What's best for Chris is to be a normal Shiba Inu and have a normal family life as a pet. Do you understand?"

Mayuka bit her lip but nodded. Then Hinata asked, "Grandpa, are you saying Chris's former owner, Mr. Kobayashi…?"

He couldn't finish the question. Sometimes Chris's ears pricked up while they were talking, as though the dog could understand human speech. Maybe some questions were better left unspoken.

Shunya lifted his eyes to gaze out the living room window.

"All I can tell you is that we don't know where he is. We can only pray that he's still safe…"

Hinata continued to eat his cake in silence. He loved Mont Blancs, but thinking about the harrowing experience Chris and Mr. Kobayashi had been through left it tasting almost sour in his mouth. Even the usually chatty Mayuka sat still and drank her juice in silence. Eventually, however, she couldn't help but ask a question.

"What kind of case is it…?"

"It's under investigation, so I can't tell anyone outside the police force. But also, I'm not an officer, so I don't know many details to begin with. If they solve the case and Kobayashi comes back, I'll be able to tell you someday."

"It sounds really bad, though I guess I can't say for sure," Mayuka muttered, lifting her feet off the floor and kicking them back and forth.

"That's all right. Mayuka, Hinata, all you need to do is be good friends to Chris… You don't have to worry about all the grown-up stuff," Shunya said. He rose from his chair. "Well, I suppose I should get going. My dogs are waiting for their walk as we speak."

After Shunya left, Hinata took Chris out for a walk of his own. Mayuka tagged along, stopping by her house along the way to drop off her school bag.

"It was hard to understand what your grandpa was talking

about back there. But basically, he wants Chris to be a normal dog and not stand out, right? Because we don't want the bad guys to come after him."

"I think so," Hinata murmured uncertainly. He had been mulling over his grandfather's words this whole time.

"But when we were searching for the owner of the earbud, Chris was really into it, right?" said Mayuka. "Like he was happy to be back on the job."

That brought Hinata back out of his thoughts. It was something he had noticed, too. When he had cowered in fear at the sight of so many police cars the previous morning, Chris had barked to cheer him up. Chris had proactively sniffed at the earbud and followed the scent all the way from the shrine. And then Chris had figured out the owner's identity and gone to the door of Takaki's apartment.

At each of those moments, Chris's eyes had been shining with life and excitement. He was the very image of a dog proud of doing a good job. And Chris was so talented!

"Chris really is remarkable," said Hinata. "If it weren't for that weird case, he'd still be doing a great job. I know it."

Chris's head perked up at the comment, as if to say, "Yes, I would!"

"It's just too bad," said Mayuka, kicking at a pebble near her foot. She turned to Hinata and asked, "Hey, can I hold the leash now?"

Hinata stopped and considered this. It had been nearly

two weeks since Chris had come to live with them. Mayuka had been present for nearly all their walks, so it would probably be safe by now.

"Okay…"

He held out the red leash to Mayuka.

"Wow! Really? It's all right?" she exclaimed, bouncing up and down. The sudden motion alarmed Chris, who took a step back.

"Hmm, I've changed my mind. I can't hand over the leash to someone who's going to startle Chris like that," he said, withdrawing his offer. He tried to continue walking, but Mayuka grabbed his arm with both hands and pulled.

"I-I'm sorry!" she whispered loudly. "I won't shout like that again. I won't jump, either. I promise—just let me hold the leash."

Well, I guess it's okay, Hinata thought reluctantly, and he handed it over.

"Okay. I'll do better this time," she said, her face serious. Chris glanced at Hinata, then walked over to Mayuka's left side with practiced ease, accepting the change in control. Hinata thought the gesture was very professional.

"R-ready, Chris? Here goes," Mayuka said, awkwardly beginning to walk. Chris matched her pace. It was clear to Hinata that Mayuka was feeling especially self-conscious. Almost immediately, she tripped over her own feet.

"Oh!" Mayuka and Hinata cried at the same time. Chris

was startled, too, but stayed in place, waiting patiently for her to get up. When she took another step forward, her arms were swinging with the same foot, rather than alternating.

Hinata burst out laughing. "Just walk like a normal person! You don't have to get so nervous."

Mayuka's cheek twitched anxiously.

"C'mon, Mayuka! Just relax, take it easy…"

Chris came to a stop, leaned over, and began to lick Mayuka's hand. She let out a deep breath, crouched, and hugged Chris around the neck. "I'm sorry, Chris. I'm still no good at walks…"

This time, Chris licked Mayuka's cheek. Hinata chuckled and took the leash back from her.

"Good try, Mayuka. Maybe tomorrow. I'm sure you'll get used to it."

She got to her feet, looked him right in the eye, and said passionately, "Doing all these things on your own, Hinata—taking in a dog, giving him walks, feeding him—it's not easy! You've gotten so used to handling Chris in just two weeks. That's incredible!"

"Now you're exaggerating," he said, blushing a little. Chris was wagging his tail rapidly, as if agreeing with Mayuka's point. Hinata grinned, then squeezed the leash with renewed focus. "All right, let's continue the walk. Where were we going?"

"I think we should go to Takaki's apartment. I wonder

what happened after we saw him last? Did he make up with Miss Rinka?"

As it happened, things were not well with Takaki at all.

When the three of them passed by his apartment building, they saw him standing in a daze outside his unit with the door wide open. He had on a heavy-looking backpack, so he might have been coming back from class.

"Um...Takaki?" Mayuka said. At the sound of her voice, he twitched and jumped ten centimeters into the air. When he craned his neck to look at her, his face was pale. Even his bleached hair, usually spiky, looked a little wilted.

"...Oh, Chris," he said.

The sight of the dog seemed to calm him for a moment. He realized it was just "Chris and Friends" and relaxed. The moment of relief cut through the tension keeping him upright, however, and he doubled over, hands on his knees, and heaved a sigh.

"What happened?" Mayuka asked, taking a step closer to him.

But Takaki straightened up and waved his hands to keep her away. "N-nothing! Nothing! Nothing at all..."

"I can tell it's not 'nothing' by the look on your face. Did something happen inside...?" she asked, rudely peering around Takaki into the apartment. That was when she saw it.

"Aaah!" she shouted, turning to Hinata. "B-b-burglar! There was a burglary!"

A burglar?! Hinata froze, but he felt himself being pulled closer. It was Chris, who had started walking toward the doorway.

"H-hey! Don't—" Takaki said, but Hinata and Chris had already seen inside.

In the kitchen just past the entryway, chairs were toppled on the floor, and pots and frying pans were strewn about. Mugs were knocked over, and pieces of plates were scattered on the ground. The refrigerator door was wide open, and plastic bottles and containers of food had been pulled out. The microwave was on the floor, its door bent at an odd angle.

In the room beyond the kitchen, blankets and clothing were tossed all over, and the sliding door of the closet had been pulled out of place so that it rested against the TV. The curtains on the back window were all torn up.

But the most shocking thing of all was on the table: a big kitchen knife stuck right into the surface!

Hinata shivered and backed away. Mayuka had already fled past the concrete wall surrounding the building and was timidly peering around the side.

"I told you not to look," Takaki said, grabbing Hinata's arm and pulling him back.

"B-but," Hinata stammered, "it's such a mess… I-I-I'll go report this to the local station…"

Takaki pulled harder, dragging Hinata all the way back to Mayuka. Chris had no choice but to follow. Once they were out on the road, the young man let go and spread out his hands. "It's nothing. Really. I'm fine. So just leave me alone and don't tell anyone else. Definitely don't go to the police! Just go."

He spun around, fled back into his apartment, and slammed the door. The sound of a heavy click made it clear he had locked them out.

Hinata and Mayuka were stunned. All they could do was look at each other.

"Wh-what...*was* that?" Mayuka asked, her voice trembling. Hinata's knees were knocking.

"It was totally ransacked," he said. "The knife...the knife stuck in the table... Did you see it, too?"

Mayuka bit her lip and nodded. "Shouldn't we go to the station...and tell Officer Iwata about it...?"

"B-but Mr. Takaki said not to," Hinata reminded her, thinking as hard as he could.

Anyone could see that someone had wrecked Takaki's apartment. But Takaki wanted to hide it. Didn't they have an obligation to report the incident to the police, now that they'd seen it for themselves? A crime had obviously occurred.

Or had one of Takaki's friends done it as some kind of mean joke? Would telling the police only turn a prank between friends into real trouble?

Still, the result had been horrible. The plates and microwave were destroyed, and the knife stuck in the table didn't seem like a fun practical joke.

Mayuka clearly agreed. "I think we *should* go see Officer Iwata..."

She started marching off, and Hinata hurried after her, pulling on Chris's leash. "What will we say? Mr. Takaki told us not to tell anyone..."

"I'm not sure. I just know I can't pretend I didn't see anything…"

She was right, but…

Mayuka stomped off. Hinata didn't have a better plan, so he just followed. Soon, the station was in sight, as was Officer Iwata, who was standing out in front. Suddenly, Mayuka stopped and turned around to face Hinata.

"You tell him, Hinata! I don't know what to say…"

That was exactly my point! he thought. Hinata pursed his lips, thinking hard.

"Please, Hinata!" She circled around behind him and pushed his back. He did his best to resist her efforts, but the motion caught Officer Iwata's attention.

"Aha! Mayuka, Hinata! How is Chris?"

Oh no, he spotted us… Hinata hung back, but Chris trotted over to Iwata. In the end, the dog pulled Hinata until he was standing right in front of the patrol officer.

"Ummm… H-hello…"

"Hi there. What's wrong? You don't look so good," the man said, his eyes kind.

Hinata breathed in and out a few times. "Umm, so… l-let's say, for example…"

"Yes?" said Officer Iwata. He crouched so he could look Hinata in the eyes.

"Uh…"

Hinata was briefly at a loss for words, until Chris gave a

little yip of encouragement. That emboldened him, and he began to speak carefully.

"L-let's say you happened to see inside someone's home. And it was really messed up... You'd be surprised and wonder if they got robbed, right?"

Iwata nodded his head, listening thoughtfully. Hinata exhaled.

"B-but if the person who lived there said it was fine and not to tell anyone...um, wh-what should you do in that situation?"

The officer straightened up and put a hand on his hat. "Mmm, that's a tough one. In my experience visiting people's homes in the area, they can be pretty cluttered. You know, when you're living in the same place for years and years, you build up lots of junk and stuff. Or maybe someone's just bad at tidying up. Is this different from that?"

It probably is, Hinata thought, remembering the sight of the knife stuck into the table. He was trying to think of what to say next when Iwata smiled and continued, "I can tell you're worried about this person, because you've got a good heart. But the most important thing, I suppose, is what *they* think. Do they want help with their problem, or do they think it's nothing and just want to be left alone?"

Oof. That stopped Hinata in his tracks. It was exactly what Takaki had said: *"It's nothing. Really. I'm fine. So just leave me alone."*

Mayuka was grimacing, too; she was clearly remembering the same thing.

But maybe it was one of those situations where he was telling them to leave it alone, but he secretly wanted help. Hinata felt that was a possibility, but he didn't know for sure, so he couldn't say anything.

"What if you just wait a little longer? I'm sure that if this person is really in need, they'll seek out help," Iwata said. He looked up at the sky for a moment, then back to Hinata. "Hang on. Are you talking about a child or a grown-up?"

Hinata and Mayuka shared a look. Mayuka hesitated but answered, "It's…a grown-up, I think."

"I see. Someone young, then," the officer said knowingly. "But if we're talking about an adult, they'll be fine. I imagine they can decide things for themselves. If it were a child, we might need to reach out a helping hand."

Hinata and Mayuka felt a bit relieved to hear this. Takaki was a college student, after all, and grown-ups could take care of themselves. This wasn't something for children to worry about.

"Thank you, Officer Iwata. Well…we should continue our walk," Hinata said, feeling better. Iwata patted him and Mayuka on the shoulder.

"Glad to hear it. You two looked pretty gloomy. You were worrying me. Have a nice walk, Chris. Take care of Hinata and Mayuka, y'hear? You're a smart dog. Oops! Sorry, some-one's calling."

He removed his smartphone from his shirt pocket to take the incoming call. Then he waved to them as he walked back into the station.

In a better mood now, Hinata and Mayuka wandered over toward Tenso Shrine with Chris.

"Officer Iwata is so nice," said Mayuka. "He really listens, even to kids like us."

Hinata agreed. "Yeah. He even talked to Chris!"

"He loves dogs. And he said Chris was smart…" Just then, Mayuka came to an abrupt stop. Something had occurred to her. "Yeah! Chris *is* smart! So I think…"

Hinata was getting a bad feeling about this. What was Mayuka thinking?

She hopped up and down, clearly enamored with this new idea of hers. "I think we should have Chris figure out who messed up Takaki's apartment. If he wants us to leave him alone, then we can do just that and solve it all on our own!"

"H-hang on, though. Grandpa said…," Hinata stammered. His grandfather had said Chris would be happier leading a normal life as a simple pet. And that was less than an hour ago!

"I know, I know. But remember how excited Chris seemed when he was tracking that scent? We have to give Chris a chance to use his skills now and then. Life isn't fun if you're just being lazy all the time."

"But how will we find the culprit…?" Hinata argued back.

"Well, first of all, we don't even know if we can. Plus, since it was probably an adult who did it, we can't arrest them on our own. So if we figure anything out, we'll just tell Officer Iwata about it."

Hinata was about to protest again when Chris barked. The timing was so perfect that it was like Chris had heard both his and Mayuka's opinions and was chiming in with his own thoughts.

"See? Chris wants to do it," Mayuka said smugly. She turned to Chris, inclined her head, and said in a high-pitched voice, "Right?"

Chris wagged his tail harder and barked again. It was like he was saying, "We're partners! Let's solve this case together!" Hinata decided he'd heard enough.

"All right, Chris. Let's give it a try… But this *has* to be a secret from Mr. Takaki, okay, Mayuka? If it seems like he might find out, we're stopping right away. And if we find some clue pointing to the culprit, we're not going to do anything about it, except let Officer Iwata know. Got it?"

Mayuka agreed, and they turned back. They had to pass the police station again, but Officer Iwata was still inside on the phone.

They turned down the narrow road leading to Takaki's apartment building, proceeding carefully to avoid drawing attention. Mayuka leaned around the side of the concrete wall to get a good look. She turned back to Hinata and mouthed the words *all clear*, so Hinata led Chris quietly into the apartment lot.

Mayuka was already inside the block fence, ear pressed boldly to Takaki's door. She listened for a while, then came back to Hinata and whispered, "It sounds like he's cleaning up in there."

Hinata nodded. Even from where he was standing, he could hear clanking, thumping, and rattling coming from inside. Takaki was doing his best to tidy up everything that had been ransacked.

The three of them should be safe for the time being. Hinata crept up to the concrete porch in front of the door, heart thumping in his chest. Chris began to sniff the air.

They could clearly see a number of whitish footprints on the ground, though their shapes were uncertain. There was about three meters of dirt between the road and the porch, and someone had probably tracked some onto the concrete, where it dried.

Some of the prints, of course, must have belonged to Takaki, as well as to Hinata and Mayuka. They couldn't be sure any of them belonged to the culprit.

And they didn't have time to stand there and think. Takaki might open the door and step out at any moment. The pounding in Hinata's chest was getting louder, and he was starting to panic. But then he noticed some large footprints beneath the small window looking into the apartment's kitchen.

He could see prints from both feet, but strangely, they were facing the road, splayed open, suggesting that the person who left them had been standing with their back toward the apartment wall. Ordinarily, there would be no reason for someone to stand there, facing that direction. Which meant...

"Maybe it was more than one person," Hinata murmured. Someone could have waited outside, keeping watch, while another person went inside and tore the place up. Chris's eyes were sparkling, telling Hinata that he was onto something.

He pointed at the footprints and quietly ordered, "Smell."

Chris sniffed at the prints vigorously. After a few moments, he looked up at Hinata.

"Now search."

Chris started walking out toward the road, snout close to the ground. Mayuka followed behind, her cheeks flushed with excitement. "You're amazing, Chris," she said. "Have you already figured out where the burglar went?"

The Shiba Inu turned left and proceeded without

hesitation, taking Mayuka and Hinata farther away from the police station.

Now Hinata's heart raced with a different kind of excitement as he held the leash. He glanced back and saw that Mayuka's ears were completely red. She looked exhilarated.

After a little while, they came to a small intersection and turned left again. There was a larger road ahead, one big enough for cars to pass through. Chris marched down the road and turned left yet again before coming to a stop. He sniffed around the area for a bit, then plopped down and stared at Hinata, whimpering. The round white eyebrows over his eyes knit together, and he looked sad.

"What's wrong, Chris? Did you lose the scent?" Mayuka asked, crouching. Hinata could imagine the sequence of events, though. After ransacking the apartment, the culprits rushed over here, and then…

"He didn't lose the scent. This is where the trail stops. I'm guessing the culprits got into a car here," he said, then glanced down the road.

They had traveled around in a square, so the main street with the police station was now ahead of them. Perhaps the ransackers had stopped their car here to avoid the police. That might mean there was a driver, too, expanding the group to three or more members. Just as Hinata had suspected, this was something much too big for two kids to handle alone.

He felt a bit relieved, but Mayuka seemed disappointed.

"So we don't know where they went from here?" she said. "That's too bad…"

Hinata laughed a little and glanced at Chris. "I don't think you're the most disappointed one here, Mayuka."

The Shiba Inu was sitting on the sidewalk, staring down the street and whining repeatedly.

5

The Swallowed Golden Star

The next day was Tuesday.

On the way home from school, Mayuka said she'd come along on Chris's walk that day.

"Don't you have English tutoring?" said Hinata. "You shouldn't skip your lesson."

Mayuka huffed and turned up her nose. "It's fine. I switched to a five-thirty class."

"That won't cause problems?"

"Not at all. My parents already okayed it. Besides, I'd rather spend time with Chris."

In fact, Mayuka was supposed to go straight home after school, so things were definitely not as okay as she was implying. Hinata was just about to say as much, when Mayuka, who was already peering into the Marron Veterinary Clinic, cried out.

"Hinata! Miss Sakurako's inside!" She yanked the door open.

He panicked. "Be careful, Mayuka, or the pets will esca—"

But she had already bounded into the lobby, crying, "I'm so glad you're feeling better!"

When Hinata entered the room, he saw Sakurako sitting on the sofa, with Mayuka standing before her and shaking her hand back and forth with both arms. Latte was sitting on Sakurako's lap, yapping with alarm at the disturbance.

"Thank you, Mayuka. I'm sorry to have worried you," Sakurako said with a smile, scooping up Latte with her left arm. She seemed tired.

Mayuka let go of her hand and beamed. "The break-in was surprising enough, but when I heard you went to the hospital, I was shocked. I'm glad you're out now. I just hope you can get the shop open again…"

The older woman gave her a noncommittal smile. "I don't know where to start… But I suppose the first thing to do will be to clean up everything that's broken. They took all of my products. I just feel so tired…"

Rui Takeuchi was sitting on the sofa next to her. He peered into Sakurako's face. "You shouldn't rush into anything. You only got out of the hospital today…"

"Rui! You're here, too?" Mayuka exclaimed, wide-eyed. She was so focused on Sakurako that she hadn't noticed him sitting there.

"I saw some blood in Chachamaru's stool, so I'm having the doctor examine him. You should just relax for now, Miss Sakurako. My grandma said she would pay you a visit."

"Thank you… Say hello to her for me."

"She's going to bring you some of those plum sweets you love so much. She said you would feel better after having something sugary with your tea."

"…Oh, that's so sweet. I think I might cry," she said, lowering her head and wiping her tears away on Latte's back. The Chihuahua fidgeted, annoyed. Sakurako sniffled and said in a hoarse voice, "The truth is, I should apologize to your grandmother… She left her emerald ring with me, and…"

"You mean the ring she was having you appraise?" Rui asked.

Sakurako hesitated, then admitted, "That's right. It was stolen, too… And it was very important to her. I feel so ashamed. I don't know how I can possibly apologize…"

Rui seemed surprised by this. He shook his head, then pushed his glasses back up before they could fall off. "There's nothing for you to apologize about. It was the burglars who did this—you're the victim, Miss Sakurako. I know that old ring well. My grandma said it was a present from my late grandfather, but I bet it wasn't worth very much. She always laughed it off and said that it was probably just colored glass."

Sakurako looked pained. "That's not true. It was very important to her, I'm sure. I feel awful. I'm so sorry…"

She started to sob. Rui, who was always so calm and collected, began to panic. "I-it's all right, Miss Sakurako. Please don't cry…"

Hinata and Mayuka were speechless. All they could do was stand and watch. At that point, the door to the examination room opened, and Suzune appeared with Chachamaru. Yuusuke popped his head out of the doorway, too.

"Thanks for waiting, Rui. Chachamaru's stool just got a little too hard, and it cut the skin when it came out. There's nothing else wrong with him," she explained. Then she sensed the strange mood in the waiting room. "What? What is it? Oh! Miss Sakurako!"

She foisted Chachamaru off on her husband and rushed over to Sakurako.

"Are you feeling all right? Maybe it was too early to ask you to come pick up Latte. Don't overexert yourself—you should probably be resting at home."

The elderly woman hid her face against Rui's shoulder, sobbing like a child. "Wh-when I'm alone, I feel like the burglars are going to come in again at any moment. I'm just terrified, and Latte can't help… I don't even want to go home anymore."

Everyone else looked at one another, unsure of what to do.

"Well, this is a problem," Suzune said, straightening up and putting a hand on the back of her neck. "Miss Sakurako isn't going to get any good rest here, and there will be other people bringing in their pets to deal with."

Rui was holding Sakurako's shoulder with one hand; he raised the other one and said, "Do you think…I should take Miss Sakurako home with me? My grandma's there, so she'll have a friend to stay with."

"Are you sure, Rui? That would be very kind of you…"

"It's fine. It sounds like nothing's wrong with Chachamaru, and I'm sure my grandma would be happy to see Miss Sakurako…"

Yuusuke nodded to Rui, still holding the cat. "Thanks a lot, Rui. We'll keep Chachamaru here for now. Don't worry—I'll take him over to your house later."

"Thank you, sir. Come with me, Miss Sakurako. Can you walk?"

The elderly woman got to her feet, apologizing over and over. With Rui helping to steady her against his shoulder, she headed for the entrance. Latte obediently trotted along after them with the pull of the leash.

Once the glass outer door had closed, the tension in the waiting room eased, and everyone exhaled together.

"Why did I have to open my big mouth and say that, about hoping she could reopen the shop?" lamented Mayuka, covering her mouth with her hands.

"You meant it to cheer her up," Suzune reassured her.

"There's not much we can do. And you can't blame her for not being over the shock of it yet."

Yuusuke nodded pensively. "Yes. It only happened two days ago, and these things take time to get over. She's got her son, but we need to support her, too... I'm glad Rui was here to help out. He's such a good kid!"

Mayuka rubbed at her eye. "Miss Sakurako's always so wonderful and mature. Watching her crying like a little kid... It felt like I was seeing a completely different person..."

"It's very difficult running a business all on your own. We've done what we could to cheer her on in the past, but after an event like this, anyone would feel broken inside."

"Do you think she'll feel better if the thieves get caught?" Mayuka asked hopefully. "Maybe if she gets all her stolen jewelry back, she'll feel a rush of motivation to keep going."

Yuusuke shifted his grip on Chachamaru and shook his head. "From what she was saying, they still don't have a lead on whoever broke in. So it was probably a group of professional thieves. And guys like that aren't going to leave clues behind."

"But we have Chris!" Mayuka protested, pointing through the ceiling to the upstairs apartment. "Chris is an excellent police dog. He'll find the trail that leads right to the bad guys!"

Hinata's mouth fell open in shock. His mother just crossed

her arms and murmured, "The whole police force is having trouble getting to the bottom of this one, so I don't see what one little dog like Chris can do."

"But," Mayuka protested, pouting.

"It's best to let the police catch the thieves; that's their job," said Yuusuke, wagging a finger. "They might have a breakthrough yet. And we're not professionals. What we *can* and *should* do is find a way to help Miss Sakurako get back on her feet."

Reluctantly, Mayuka agreed. Hinata was relieved that she had decided to drop the matter. He picked up her backpack and said, "C'mon, Mayuka. Let's take Chris for a walk. We're running out of time."

"Okay…"

They were just turning toward the automatic door when someone came rushing up to the clinic, pulled open the glass door to the outside, and hurried in. Hinata and Mayuka jumped out of the way.

"Doctor! Dr. Suzune, please help!"

It was Yukina, carrying her dog Linda in her arms, clearly in a panic.

"What's the matter, Yukina?" Suzune asked.

"It's Linda! Linda found some…something *weird*, and…!"

"Now, now, calm down. Just relax, catch your breath, and explain. What happened to Linda?"

Panting, Yukina handed Linda to the vet. For her part,

Linda seemed surprised but otherwise normal. Suzune was nonplussed.

"She seems fine to me."

"N-no! I mean, she's fine now, but earlier, she ate something weird, and…"

Suzune frowned. "She ate something she shouldn't have? What was it?"

"I don't know. We were on a walk, when… Oh! Do you know where Tenso Shrine is?"

The doctor nodded, prompting her to continue.

"Well, I went there to pray, but Linda got under the

offering box and started scratching. I saw something shiny stuck on her paw. Then she got it in her mouth…"

"And when you tried to take it away, she swallowed it," Suzune finished, much to Yukina's surprise.

"Did you see it happen, Doctor?"

"No, it's just very common. Dogs think you're trying to steal their prey, so they hurry to swallow it. How big was the object?"

Yukina made a face. "It was golden, not that big… I really don't know! It all happened so fast."

Suzune adjusted Linda in her arms and opened the door to the exam room. "Yuusuke, can you prep the X-ray machine? Wait right there, Yukina. I want to identify what it is first before we decide on a course of action… We might need to take it out with an endoscope. Or in the worst-case scenario, perform surgery to extract the object."

Suddenly, the waiting room was tense again.

Yuusuke promptly followed Suzune into the exam area. Yukina, meanwhile, slumped to the floor weakly.

"S-surgery…?"

Mayuka crouched next to her and said soothingly, "Don't worry, Yukina. I'm sure it'll turn out fine. I bet it's nothing…"

But Yukina put her hands on her cheeks and shook her head back and forth. "I'm so, so stupid! I was so focused on praying that I completely stopped paying attention to Linda…"

"Praying? It must have been about something really important."

"No, it wasn't! I was just hoping to win a drawing for some concert tickets. I'm so mad at myself. It wasn't important at all. And if something happens to Linda…"

Yukina started to wail, much to Mayuka's consternation.

"D-don't cry… I'm sure it'll be fine…," the younger girl said unconvincingly. She looked to Hinata for help. He just shook his head. At times like this, there was nothing you could say. All they could do was wait for the diagnosis to come back.

What an exhausting day this has been, Hinata thought, sighing. *Two separate people bursting into tears in the lobby. Poor Chris is probably upstairs wondering when I'm going to get home…*

For a while, the only sound was Yukina's quiet sobbing. Hinata and Mayuka kept glancing at each other as they waited for the door to the examination room to open again.

Hinata was looking at the ceiling, thinking about Chris, when Suzune emerged at last. "Thanks for waiting, Yukina," she said, wiping her hands with a paper towel.

"H-how is it, Doctor?" Yukina asked, springing to her feet.

"From what I can see on the X-ray, there *is* an object in her stomach. It's probably made of metal. We could try getting her to throw it up, but the shape will make it a little tricky."

"What shape?"

"It looks like a classic five-pointed star. If we induce vomiting, the pointy ends might damage her esophagus. But I think if we put a tube down her throat, we can get the object out. In other words, an endoscopy. It'll require putting her under, but it's much less invasive than cutting her open."

Yukina slapped her knees and exhaled heavily. "Thank goodness. So Linda will be all right?"

"She'll be fine. We'll handle it," Suzune said with a reassuring thumbs-up. Yukina thanked her profusely.

"Wow, Linda's kind of a dummy. Who'd eat something off the ground like that?" Mayuka said without thinking. Hinata yanked on her arm. *How rude!*

But Yukina just wiped away her tears and said, "Yeah, Linda's a dummy… But that's what makes her so adorable."

"It's a common thing with dogs," said Suzune wisely. "They just love to eat things they find on the ground."

Mayuka was surprised by this. "Even Chris?"

"Chris has formal training, so he's a little different. Anyway, I should get ready for the endoscopy. This is still a surgical procedure, Yukina, so you should call home and let everyone know," Suzune said before returning to the exam room.

Yukina sat down on the sofa, clearly feeling better now, and took out her phone.

Mayuka turned to Hinata. "I'm glad it's—…"

That was when she noticed that his lips were pursed, and he was staring motionless at the ceiling.

"Hinata…?" she said cautiously. But his eyes remained glued to a single spot. "Hinata! Hellooo? What's going on?"

Only by raising her voice did she finally draw his attention away.

"Oh, sorry," he said. "I was thinking about something. Oh yeah, since Linda seems to be fine, we should go take Chris for that walk. It's getting late."

He got up, suddenly restless, and hurried for the automatic door. Mayuka scurried after him.

"Wait up! I'm coming with you!"

"What was it that stuck out to you?" Mayuka asked as they walked Chris. Hinata was looking straight ahead, marching them across the shopping area toward the police station. He was going faster than usual, which seemed to be making even Chris a little nervous.

"Tenso Shrine, the offering box…," he muttered under his breath.

Mayuka was taken aback. "Huh? You mean the place where Linda ate the weird object? What about it?"

"…And a star-shaped item. Put those three things together. Does it remind you of anything?"

Mayuka kept up with Hinata's pace, thinking hard. After crossing at the light, Hinata turned right and made straight for the Shinto shrine in the distance.

Once they'd passed through the red torii gate and entered the grounds, Hinata paused to examine the area. It was quiet and empty.

They continued down the stone path, then up the stairs. Hinata put his hands together to pray before the shrine.

"Dear God, please excuse me, but I need to see the underside of the offering box…"

He bowed deeply, then bent his knees and crouched to look under the box.

"What are you doing, Hinata?" Mayuka asked, joining him on the ground. Chris started sniffing around the area, too.

There was a gap of about five centimeters between the bottom of the box and the ground. Hinata got his head all the way down to peer into the gap, but it was too dark to see anything. He gave up, stood, and handed the leash to Mayuka.

"Take Chris for a moment."

Mayuka did so without complaint. Chris looked back and forth between Hinata and Mayuka, mystified.

Hinata got down on the paving stone again and reached under the offering box. It was a meter wide and about sixty centimeters deep. He felt around, searching left and right for anything he could grab. His arm wasn't long enough to reach the back, so by the end he'd lain down on his stomach.

"What are you searching for, Hinata? Are you sure about this? Your hands and clothes are getting all dirty!" Mayuka said with obvious concern. Chris just watched.

Just as Hinata's hand got as far back as it could reach, his fingertips brushed against something. He strained to get farther, grabbed the object, and pulled it out.

"What is that?"

Mayuka leaned in to examine the item in Hinata's hand as he got to his feet.

It was a black bag—a shoulder bag, with a golden fastener.

"Oh!" she gasped. Hinata patted it and brushed the dust off.

"I-isn't that Takaki's?" Mayuka asked. "The bag that he said got stolen near the station?"

"I think so…," Hinata murmured, pulling the golden zipper to check inside. It was empty. Scratch that—there was a single pack of tissues, wrapped in an advertisement for a karaoke place.

Hinata put the tissues back and asked Mayuka, "Mr. Taka-ki's stolen bag matched Miss Rinka's, right?"

She nodded.

He continued, "And Miss Rinka had a golden star charm attached to her zipper, didn't she?"

"Oh, yeah, she did. But there isn't one on this—... Oh! Do you think the star that fell off this one is what Linda swallowed?"

Hinata bobbed his head. "When my mom said there was a star-shaped metal object on the X-ray, I thought, just maybe, we might find Mr. Takaki's bag here."

"But...but...," Mayuka stammered, putting her hands over her head. The gesture pulled the leash up a little, annoy-ing Chris, who was forced to trot a step or two toward her. "The bag was stolen outside the station, right? Why is it here? And this is where Takaki dropped his earbud, so he must have been here, too! What does it mean?!"

"Maybe Mr. Takaki's bag wasn't stolen. Maybe he hid it himself."

"You mean he lied about it being stolen?"

"...Yeah."

"What? But this bag was a birthday present from Miss Rinka, wasn't it? It should be really important to him! Why would he lie and hide it?"

They looked at the black shoulder bag for a good while. Chris was glancing at them with apparent concern.

"What should we do with the bag? Give it back to Takaki?" Mayuka asked hesitantly.

"Hmmm," Hinata murmured. "If Mr. Takaki hid it here on his own, that means he didn't want it found, right?"

"Should we take it to Officer Iwata, then?"

"You only turn things in to the police if you don't know who the owner is, right? And we already *know* this bag is Mr. Takaki's."

"Ugh, this is so confusing… I know! Let's hide it under the offering box again!"

Hinata couldn't believe what he was hearing. "We can't do that! We found it. We can't just pretend we didn't."

"Oh, you're such a Goody Two-shoes, Hinata," said Mayuka. Chris barked, as if to say that was one of Hinata's good points. The kids giggled.

"How about this?" Hinata suggested. "Since we've already found it, I don't want to pretend like we didn't. So what if we go hang it on Mr. Takaki's doorknob without saying anything. Like Officer Iwata said, Mr. Takaki is a grown-up, so he can decide what to do about it."

"Yeah, that's a good idea! Plus, it was a present, so I think he should have it."

With that decision made, they rushed back to the shrine gate.

"Mayuka, you're giving Chris a proper walk!" Hinata said as they ran.

She looked at the leash, which was still in her hand, and realized what she'd done.

"You're right! As long as I don't overthink it, it's actually pretty easy!"

Chris looked up at Mayuka as he ran and barked happily.

The police station was empty. There was only a sign on the desk that read OUT ON PATROL. Hinata felt a bit like they were doing things behind Officer Iwata's back and was relieved he was gone.

Then, just as they turned the corner toward Takaki's apartment building, they nearly ran into someone coming the other way.

"Oh! I'm sorry!" Mayuka said—then gasped.

It was Takaki and Rinka.

Instantly, Rinka was pointing. "Oh! There! That's the bag I gave you!"

Hinata squeezed the bag against his chest and hunched his shoulders guiltily. Their plan to silently leave the bag at his place had just gone up in smoke.

"But why do you have it? Where was it?" Rinka asked, her eyes wide as she took the shoulder bag from Hinata to examine it.

Mayuka froze in place. Takaki's face had gone completely blank.

Hinata's mind was racing as fast as it possibly could. What should he say…? How would he explain the series of events that had led to them finding the bag?

Chris whined briefly, encouraging him, and that was enough. "Um, m-my family runs a veterinary clinic…," Hinata said.

"Oh, really? And what does that have to do with this bag?" Rinka asked, perplexed.

Hinata had to make a decision. And he decided it would be best to tell as much of the truth as possible. Once you started to lie, you had to commit to it, and you'd end up telling even more lies to cover it up.

Clumsily, he did his best to explain. Someone came to the clinic with a dog that had eaten something it shouldn't have while on a walk. The object had been underneath the offering box at the shrine. An X-ray had shown that it was shaped like a star. And he'd remembered that Rinka's bag had a star-shaped charm hanging from the zipper…

"T-Takaki's bag matches yours, isn't that what you said? So it would have had the same star charm. I wondered if the thief tossed it underneath the offering box at the shrine. Then the charm came off, and the dog swallowed it, or something like that…"

Rinka's big eyes blinked, her long eyelashes fluttering. "So you looked under the offering box and found it there? That's amazing! You're like a pair of kid detectives!" She spun around and held out the bag to the still-dazed Takaki. "Look! They found it for you, so take good care of it this time. Don't you dare let it get stolen again!"

The pressure of the bag against his chest woke Takaki from his daze. His face, however, was noticeably pale.

"Y-yeah," he stammered unconvincingly. She smacked him on the arm.

"Make sure you thank them. These kids just got your bag back."

"Th-thanks, guys… You've been a huge help," he said with great effort. Then he slipped his backpack off, bent over, and opened the zipper so he could stuff his bag inside.

"What are you doing?" Rinka asked suspiciously. Takaki zipped up his backpack, looking around nervously before straightening up again.

"It's, uh, really important to me, so I wanted to stash it away for safekeeping… Okay, see you."

He started speed-walking toward the traffic light.

"Ugh, why are you being so weird?" Rinka snapped, sticking out her tongue in his direction. She turned to the kids. "I'm sorry about that. Thank you so much. Oh! I know what to do," she said, grinning. "I'm actually pretty good at handiwork, like crafts and baking. Why don't I whip you up some delicious homemade cookies next time? Right now I've gotta go. Takaki and I are supposed to get ramen by the station before he goes to work!"

Rinka waved goodbye, then hurried after her boyfriend, who was waiting at the light. She caught up to him and leaned against his arm.

"Takaki's such a weirdo. But even after all that, the two of them seem close," Mayuka commented, watching the pair. Hinata agreed, but he'd noticed something just then.

"That was the first time Mr. Takaki didn't say anything to Chris."

Who Is the Jewel Thief?

It was an overcast morning.

Hinata opened the gate to Chris's pen in the living room, rubbing his eyes.

"Good morning, Chris. How did you sleep? I didn't get much rest last night, because I was thinking too much. I barely even feel awake…"

He yawned, stretched, and put the leash on Chris's collar. Chris licked the end of Hinata's nose as if to say, "Wake up, sleepyhead."

Hinata took the dog down the stairs to the street, where he looked around the shopping district. He was so tired that he couldn't even make up his mind about whether to go right or left.

By the time they'd gotten back to the clinic the day before, Linda's surgery was over and successful. "Off you go!" Suzune had said, and Yukina left with tears of joy in her eyes, accompanied by her mother.

The star-shaped object retrieved from the dog's stomach was to be discarded along with the medical waste, so Hinata didn't get a chance to see it. He already knew that it had come off Takaki's bag, so he didn't need to see it, but he was still a little disappointed.

There was absolutely no way someone had stolen the bag from Takaki. Hinata was certain of that, based on the way Takaki had been acting.

He hadn't looked happy in the least when the stolen bag came back to him. In fact, he seemed shocked, confused, and even scared to be given something he hadn't expected to see again.

What didn't make sense yet was why he would lie and say that such an important bag was stolen, and why he would hide it in that location.

Hmmm… Hinata shook his head, trying to clear away the mental cobwebs.

"I think we should go to Tenso Shrine, Chris. Maybe we'll find a hint there," he said, turning to the right.

A woman was walking toward them from the other direction. She was tall and wearing a white suit. The clicking of her high heels was loud in the quiet street.

He had seen her before, he realized. "Good morning," he said politely.

The woman stopped and looked at him in surprise. She was very well-dressed in a way that seemed out of place for an empty street so early in the morning.

"Good morning. Do I know you?" she asked.

Hinata, too, was surprised that he had spoken to her. The old Hinata would never have had the courage. When had he ever said hello to a stranger before...?

"Um, I...I saw you outside Sakura Jewelry the other day. You were with a man..."

"Oh!" She smiled and extended her hand. "That's right. I'm the president of Chez Bijoux Helen. My name is Helen Mehito. That man is my company's jewelry designer."

Hinata timidly took her hand. She smelled nice. It was an attention-grabbing smell, just like her look. Chris would be able to follow this scent forever without losing the trail.

"Do you live here?" Helen asked, glancing at the Marron Veterinary Clinic sign. He nodded. "I see. That's a very cute dog. Well, bye, now..."

She smiled again and walked away toward the station. The clicking of her heels grew more and more distant.

Hinata just stood there, watching her go. Despite their very brief conversation, he didn't think he'd forget such a memorable person anytime soon.

That was when he noticed that Chris was also facing Helen, and *growling*. The dog's teeth were bared in a snarl.

Hinata was shocked—he had never seen Chris act like this before.

"What's the matter, Chris? She's just a pretty lady. C'mon, let's keep walking."

With the torii gate of Tenso Shrine in sight, Hinata murmured to Chris, "We sure do come here a lot these days, don't we?"

But Chris didn't seem to mind. Maybe the Shiba Inu really liked it here. At the very least, Hinata's mind was feeling clear and crisp again, so he was in good spirits as he entered the shrine grounds.

And then he stopped.

How unusual. I didn't expect to see someone at the shrine at this hour. And it's...

...Takaki! The silhouette from behind, the spiked blond hair—it had to be him. He was even wearing his usual backpack. The tall man was hunched over, glancing left and right.

Hinata quickly pulled on the leash and backed Chris behind the little structure meant for washing one's hands before praying. He got the feeling it would be a bad idea to go up to Takaki right now. Once they were hidden, he stuck just the side of his face around to get a look at the shrine.

Takaki peered under the offering box for a while, then got up and circled around the left side of the shrine building. What was he doing? Hinata ducked behind the large washing basin and considered his options. He wanted to find out what Takaki was up to, but it would be bad if the young man saw him. Still, he *really* wanted to know.

In the end, curiosity won out. He put a finger to his lips, telling Chris to be quiet, and crept around toward the shrine. Like Takaki, he went around the left side to the rear of the building.

There was a narrow empty space behind the shrine that was even more overgrown and shady than the front. Hinata sneaked over to a large tree so he could hide behind the trunk. Chris followed quietly as well, catching on to the idea.

A rustling noise nearby turned out to be Takaki making his way behind an old storage shed in the back. Hinata could hear the sound of the knee-high grass being parted and swept around. He held his breath, willing himself to stay silent, until the rustling stopped and he sensed the movement coming closer. On a sudden instinct, Hinata crouched, hugged Chris, and pulled the bright-red leash closer, keeping it out of sight.

A moment later, he heard Takaki cough somewhere very close by.

He spotted us! Hinata thought, hunching even smaller.

But the footsteps continued, passing them by. Eventually, they turned crisp and light as Takaki got back on the stone path. Then they faded away.

Oh, good! He didn't see us... Hinata let out a breath of pure relief and hugged Chris even closer. They stayed that way for a good while, hiding behind the tree. Then Hinata came back to his senses and jumped up. If they lingered here in this overgrown area, Chris was going to get spooked by bugs! They had to leave.

Hinata peeked around the side of the shrine toward the torii gate. There was no one on the path out front. He turned back to the rear area and, praying that no bugs flew over, approached the storage shed.

"Can you do it, Chris? I really want to see what's back there, so I'm going into the grass. If there are any bugs, I'll give you a hug to keep you safe. It'll only take a minute. You can do it."

Chris's eyebrows bunched up pitifully, and the dog whined, but he seemed to understand Hinata's intention. Hesitantly, the former police dog followed his owner.

The grass behind the shed was in disarray from Takaki stepping through it. Hinata examined the underside of the raised shed. About halfway back along the side of the wall, the grass was less disturbed, and there was a little bit of black fabric visible, poking out from under the shed. Hinata carefully pulled on the fabric and sighed when he saw what it was—the very same black shoulder bag he had returned to Takaki the day before.

Apparently, the young man was really intent on hiding this thing. Even though it was a present from his sweetheart, Rinka, who seemed to mean so much to him...

"It doesn't make sense, Chris. What's going on?"

Chris stuck his snout under the shed and began to sniff.

"What are you doing? If you poke around there, you're going to find some ants, or pill bugs, or..."

Then Hinata came to his senses and realized what Chris's action meant. Was there something else, too?

He peered at the spot where the bag had been and noticed another object farther back. He reached in and pulled out something rectangular wrapped in a black plastic bag. It was taped up, but there was a tear in the plastic. It was rather heavy, which made Hinata assume it was a book.

But after undoing the tape and taking out the contents, he found a large brown envelope instead. The end of the envelope was taped up, but the tape had torn open.

When he saw what was inside the envelope, Hinata was so shocked that he dropped it. The resulting thump in the grass caused Chris to jump in surprise.

Very carefully, Hinata picked up the envelope and looked again at what was inside.

"M-money..."

He had never seen so many large bills before in his life.

His heart was racing. This had to be *dirty* money. There was no other explanation for why it would be hidden in a place like this.

His knees started knocking. What should he do?

Hinata thought of Officer Iwata. This was something that *had* to be delivered to the police. But to do so would mean telling the police about Takaki. He wouldn't have come here if he weren't following Takaki and would certainly never have found this stack of bills.

Takaki must have been the one who hid the money. It was in the same place as his bag, after all.

On the other hand…while this was all very fishy, Takaki didn't seem like a bad person. Before any of this happened, he'd been bright and funny and friendly. And he loved Chris.

Should I really turn him in to the police?

"What should I do, Chris…?" he asked the dog. He was at a loss. Chris simply looked back expectantly. "Oh no! A bug…"

Hinata heard a faint buzzing right near his ear. He swung his hand around, trying to drive it off. Now he knew what to do.

"I've got it! I'll follow the Mayuka formula. I didn't see what I just saw!"

He quickly stuffed the envelope full of money and the black plastic bag into the shoulder bag, then returned it to the grass beneath the shed. Just to be sure, he kicked it farther back with his toe.

He had to get going, or he'd be late for school. But at least he'd have time throughout the day to think about what had happened.

Hinata left the grass and started jogging toward the front of the shrine. It was the same old quiet, secluded path. But his heart was racing like never before.

"I'm sorry, Chris. You didn't get much of a walk this morning."

The low canopy of clouds was breaking apart overhead, and the sun was shining through. Hinata squinted against the glare and hurried home with his dog.

But all the time in the world couldn't guarantee that he'd come up with a good idea.

Hinata felt this truth keenly on his way home from school. No matter how hard he thought, he kept running into a wall. He couldn't even discuss the issue with Mayuka, because they couldn't talk about it when people were around, and they barely had any time alone.

He couldn't remember anything said in class that day, and it felt like he hadn't eaten a bite during lunch.

"Ugh…"

He grumbled and fretted as he waited for the crossing gate next to Aoba Station to rise. Mayuka was getting worried and poked him in the side.

"Hey, what happened? You can tell me now, can't you? I knew there was something wrong when you didn't even want your carrot cake at lunch!"

Hinata had been too preoccupied with his thoughts to savor dessert, and he gave his to a friend instead. Now he regretted it a little.

The train passed, and the crossing bar rose. Hinata crossed the tracks with big strides.

"I can't talk about it outside, Mayuka. Will you come over?"

"What does that mean?" she said, looking confused. But she smacked his backpack anyway and said, "All right, I'll come over. I mean, I'm there every day anyway!"

"Are you serious?!"

Mayuka shot up from her chair with a loud thunk the moment she heard about the bundle of cash hidden under the shed behind the shrine. Her glass nearly toppled off the table.

"And Takaki hid it?" she asked. "That's not normal at all. How much was there?"

"Umm, I don't know…"

"You know how they show stacks of cash on TV shows sometimes? Where they're split up and wrapped with a little strip of paper around each one. How many of those were there?"

Hinata looked down at Chris and shook his head. "They weren't wrapped up like that, and they weren't fancy new bills, either. I don't think even you could have figured out how much was in there."

Mayuka picked up her glass and downed the rest of her soda.

"Then I'm going to check it out. Let's go to the shrine."

There was a couple—an old man and woman—praying when the three of them arrived at Tenso Shrine. Hinata, Mayuka, and Chris waited patiently for them to leave, then went around the back of the building.

"Will you watch out for any bugs, Mayuka?" Hinata asked, handing her the leash.

She nodded. "Got it. I guess it *is* pretty overgrown back here."

Hinata went first, stepping behind the shed, then Mayuka followed him into the grass with Chris. He reached under the side of the raised shed and found that the bag was still there. His heart was racing again. Summoning his courage, he pulled it out and opened the zipper. The envelope was still inside. He removed it, opened the end, and offered it to Mayuka.

She put a hand to her chest, inhaled, and looked into the envelope.

"Whoa! N-no way… I've never seen so much money."

"Right? What do you think we should do? Turn it in to the police?"

"Argh!" Mayuka exhaled dramatically. "Stupid Takaki! He must be involved in some shady business. It would probably be for the best if we told Officer Iwata and had the police arrest him. But," she said, suddenly on the verge of tears, "that would make Miss Rinka so sad, if her boyfriend got arrested…"

Of course it would, Hinata thought. *They're a couple. She'd probably be devastated. And we wouldn't feel any better. He just doesn't seem like a bad person. I don't think he's rotten to the core or anything. And that's what's been troubling me all day long.*

Mayuka sniffled and said, "Hey, Hinata, isn't it true that you get a lighter sentence if you turn yourself in?"

"Turn yourself in?"

"You know, when someone who's committed a crime goes to the police to confess what they've done."

Oh, right. Yeah, I suppose if you go to the police and confess your crimes, they might be more lenient. I think I remember learning something like that.

Hinata put the envelope back into the bag and thought things over.

"Should we return it to Takaki? And say 'Take it and go to the police'?"

Mayuka wrinkled her nose up at the shoulder bag, like she was seeing something disgusting. "We can't carry around that much cash. I'd be scared that someone would try to attack us. Can't we just talk to him?"

"…Good point. I guess we should pretend we didn't see this again."

Hinata pursed his lips and glanced at Chris, who whimpered in quiet concern. Hinata took that as agreement and pushed the bag back under the shed.

Mayuka murmured, "What do you think Takaki will say? Will he go to the police?"

Hinata shook his head. He just didn't know. He didn't even know if Takaki would talk to them. But he also thought it was the best option they had at this point.

"Let's get out of here, before the bugs find us…"

Officer Iwata was standing outside the police station as they passed by.

Hinata tensed. This was the last person he wanted to see right now. But Mayuka took Chris right up to the man.

"Hello, Officer!"

"Oh, Mayuka. Hi to you, too, Chris. What's wrong, Hinata?"

As usual, Iwata was very sharp. Hinata forced a smile and walked over to join them.

"…Nothing. I'm fine. Just a little sleepy."

"I see. Well, you'd better get to bed early tonight, then… Hmm? What is it, Mayuka?" She was poking his arm.

"Um, Officer Iwata, is it true that you get a lighter sentence if you turn yourself in?"

Hinata nearly jumped out of his skin. *Mayuka, you can't just come out and say it!*

The policeman was equally taken aback. He seemed surprised as he took a closer look at Mayuka. "Why, did you do something bad?"

She smacked his arm. "It's not about me! I'm asking in general! Since you're an expert."

He seemed truly perplexed now. "W-well, that's a very complicated question... Generally speaking, if you go to the police and admit to crimes you've committed, you are considered to have surrendered yourself," he said, speaking with a professional air. "If you've surrendered, your sentence might end up being lighter. But if the police already know you did something—say, if you're wanted—it's not counted as surrendering in the same way if you simply walk up to a station and reveal yourself. Therefore, there are times when it *won't* decrease your sentence. Does that make sense?"

Mayuka blinked as she listened, surprised by the depth of his answer. Once he finished, she composed herself enough to bow and say, "Th-thank you. I think I understand now."

"Of course, it's all case by case. There are always other factors involved. It won't always lighten a person's sentence... But in terms of expressing remorse, I think turning yourself in is important."

Mayuka nodded a few times, and Iwata grinned and waved a finger at her.

"So who's turning themselves in?"

Hinata panicked and was about to insert himself between the two of them when Mayuka shook her head and said boldly, "No one specific. I said 'in general,' didn't I? It's for homework. I'm studying about turning yourself in to the police."

Iwata reached up and adjusted his hat, laughing. "I see! They sure give kids some pretty tricky homework these days. Do you remember what I told you? Don't need to take notes or anything?"

"I'm fine. I've got a good memory," she said, pointing to her head.

The officer laughed out loud again. "Ha-ha-ha... Well, you'd better get home so you can finish your assignment. Just one thing, though," he said, suddenly serious. He looked from Mayuka to Hinata and back. "Don't get yourselves involved in anything dangerous. There's darkness like you'd never imagine in the world of grown-ups."

Cowed by his shift in tone, Hinata and Mayuka nodded to show they understood.

"Chris, if you think your owner or his friend are putting themselves in danger, you have to stop them. They're relying on you. Now! Time to get ready for my patrol."

Iwata gave Chris a pat on the head and withdrew back into the station.

"You had me sweating buckets, Mayuka," Hinata said, pouting as they headed to Takaki's apartment.

She seemed unfazed by the experience. "I just figured Officer Iwata would know about the rules of turning yourself in. And he did. Now I'm convinced we should talk Takaki into it."

But what could they say to convince him? Hinata thought Mayuka was being too optimistic. Was she really considering everything that might happen? Hinata could feel his stomach prickling with anxiety. Soon they were standing before Takaki's apartment building. Mayuka strode right up to his door.

"Ready, Hinata? I'm going to press the button."

"W-wait. Who's going to do the talking?"

"You."

A-are you kidding? I'm not...I'm not...

Hinata's mouth worked silently. Mayuka, not bothering to wait, pressed the button. *Uh-oh...*

They could hear some footsteps inside, and the door opened a crack. The chain was still on.

"Hello...?"

It was a woman's voice: Rinka's. So she was visiting Takaki's apartment. Mayuka peered through the crack.

"Miss Rinka?" she said. "It's me, Mayuka. Is Takaki there?"

"Oh, Mayuka?"

The door shut, and there was a clatter as the chain was removed. Then it opened again. Rinka was standing in the doorway, but she seemed dazed and upset. Her eyes were swollen, and there were black smudges below them, probably from crying into her mascara.

"What's wrong, Miss Rinka? Are you okay?" Mayuka asked with concern. Rinka used the T-shirt in her hand to wipe her eyes. It was one of Takaki's flashy shirts with designs that looked like paint splatters.

"Takaki left. Because I got mad at him. But...but..." She sobbed and sniffled before launching into her story. "He gave me a ring. As a birthday present. But it's a really huge one. It has a gigantic jewel in the middle, surrounded by little diamonds. There's no way he could afford something like that. It looks crazy expensive. The design is a little old-fashioned, though. I asked him why he'd give me something like that, and he said it was my birthstone, and he thought I'd like it. But I don't think Takaki even knows what birthstones are!"

She paused to take a breath and collect herself before continuing.

"He's been weird recently. Something's going on. His apartment was all messed up the day before yesterday! He said he was drinking after he got home from work and got so drunk that he wrecked the place. But that doesn't make sense, does it? I was helping him clean up all yesterday, before you kids came along… I told him I don't need jewelry—I just want the old Takaki to come back. Then he got mad and left."

Rinka buried her face in the T-shirt and sobbed. Mayuka didn't know what to do; she kept shooting glances back at Hinata.

Inside his head, a warning sign was lighting up. *What is this…? I feel like something's connecting in my mind. Something very important is almost in my grasp, but I can't get a grip on it. And if I don't grab on to it now, something terrible might happen…*

Without realizing it, Hinata started to speak.

"Miss Rinka, what's your birthstone?"

She looked up and murmured, "It's May, so…emerald…"

Emerald. He had just heard that word recently. The voice that had said it echoed in his head.

"She left her emerald ring with me, and…"

That's it! Hinata looked Rinka right in the eye.

"Do you still have the ring?" he asked.

"I do. Takaki left it here when he stormed out."

"May I see it?"

"Sure, I guess…"

Rinka went back inside, then came out with a ring

displayed in the palm of her hand. There was a translucent elliptical jewel set in a golden base. The jewel was green, and there were little diamonds embedded all around it. The ring was quite fabulous. Like Rinka said, it looked "crazy expensive."

"That's so pretty. What a big gemstone!" Mayuka said, entranced.

Hinata stared so hard, he could have burned holes in it. The voice was still speaking in his head.

"She always laughed it off and said that it was probably just colored glass."

He stared at it in silence for so long that Rinka finally asked, "Are you done yet?"

Hinata looked up. "May I take it for a little while?"

"What?"

"I want to show it to someone…"

"Who?" asked Rinka and Mayuka at the same time.

Hinata had to pause. How should he explain himself?

"T-to…um…a jewelry store owner I know. Someone who might know its value…"

"Oh, you mean Miss Sakurako?" Mayuka said excitedly. "I'll go with you!"

"You wait here with Chris, Mayuka. I'll be back very soon."

"How come?!" she exclaimed, pouting.

Hinata tried his best to placate her. "I'm borrowing a very

expensive ring from Rinka. You should stay here in its place to prove I'll come back."

Rinka giggled and handed it to him. "That's very admirable of you, Hinata. I don't believe you'd take the ring and run, though I do think it's strange that a little boy knows a jewelry store owner…"

Mayuka said proudly, "She lives in the shopping district, too. She's a very lovely old woman."

"Oh… Well, I'd be very happy if you stayed here with me, Mayuka, Chris. Could you help me take down the tattered curtains? It's so depressing being in here alone."

Mayuka glanced at Hinata, then said, "I suppose it's all right. Can Chris come inside? Do you have any napkins or wet tissues that we can use to wipe his paws?"

While Rinka went inside to get wipes, Mayuka shot Hinata a look and said, "Just be quick, okay? I'll try to investigate Takaki's apartment in the meantime."

Hinata nodded and patted Chris on the head. "Take care of Mayuka for me. I'll be back as soon as I can."

Chris yipped in understanding and turned to Mayuka. Hinata squeezed the ring into the palm of his hand and started running.

Okay, next, I need to turn by the bakery…
Hinata consulted his memory as he ran—he had delivered medicine for Chachamaru once before. The clinic had

been very busy, and his father had asked him to help out. There had been a big pine tree in front of the house, he recalled.

Once he spotted the pine tree, Hinata checked the family nameplate outside to make sure it was the right one, then pressed the intercom button below. The response was immediate.

"Hello, who is this…? Oh! Hinata!"

Moments later, the front door opened, and Rui popped his head out.

"Hurry, come in! I don't want Chachamaru to sneak outside."

He waved Hinata through the gate. Their home smelled old-fashioned, which made sense, as its owner was a tea ceremony master. The entryway was nice and clean, and there was an arrangement of purple flowers above the shoe stand just inside the door.

Rui smiled at his classmate. Half of Chachamaru's face could be seen through a door cracked open down the hall. "What brings you here, Hinata? You don't usually come over to play."

That's not why I'm here at all, Hinata thought. He swallowed and extended his hand.

"Rui… Do you recognize this?"

"Huh?"

Rui pressed a switch on the wall to turn on a light,

brightening the gloomy entryway. The ring on Hinata's palm glittered.

"Oh." Rui's mouth dropped open. "Th-that looks a lot like my grandma's ring. But it was stolen by those burglars, right? She's out at a tea ceremony right now, but if you don't mind, I'll take a look…"

He plucked the ring out of Hinata's palm, adjusted his glasses, and held the little item up to the light.

"Yes… It *is* Grandma's ring. See where it says her name?"

Hinata took the ring back with trembling fingers and held it up to the light in the same way. On the inside of the golden band was a name engraved in English letters: K-A-Z-U-E.

He felt a painful twinge in his chest. It was true. Takaki was in possession of a ring that had been stolen from Sakura Jewelry. That meant...

"How did you get this, Hinata?" Rui asked curiously. Hinata didn't know what to say. "Where did you find it?"

Hinata could only smile vaguely as he pressed the ring into Rui's hand and said quickly, "I—I can't tell you yet... But I thought it might be your grandmother's and came here to make sure. I'll be back to explain later, but for now, give that to your grandma... I'm sorry!"

He turned around and ran outside.

"Hinata!" Rui called out from behind, but Hinata ignored him and raced back through the shopping district.

7

Plunging into Darkness

"Mayuka! Miss Rinka!"

Hinata banged on the door of Takaki's apartment, breathing heavily.

"What is it, Hinata? Why are you shouting?" asked Rinka as she opened the door and shot him a funny look.

"S-sorry, Miss Rinka," he said. "I gave the ring back to its owner."

"Owner? Wait, you mean it belonged to someone else? Does that mean Takaki—?"

Hinata cut her off. "Where did he go? I need to talk to him right away. Do you have any idea where he might be?"

When she saw how serious Hinata was, Rinka's face hardened as well. "Where…? At a friend's house? School? Should I call him? If he's at work, he won't be able to pick up…"

Hinata had a sudden realization. There was one more thing he needed to figure out.

"Miss Rinka, do you know what kind of job Takaki does?"

"Nuh-uh. He won't tell me. Before he started, he was excited about it, saying that it was a pretty lucrative position, but it seems like it's really demanding…"

Mayuka and Chris popped their heads out from behind Rinka.

"Did you see Miss Sakurako, Hinata?"

"Chris!" Hinata shouted. The former police dog snapped to attention, immediately sensing the change in Hinata's attitude. Chris waited, tense, for the next command.

"Chris, can I ask you to investigate with me?" Hinata asked.

"Woof!"

"Miss Rinka, these are Mr. Takaki's sneakers, right?" he asked, pointing to some old sneakers in the entryway. She nodded, so he picked them up and stuck them right under Chris's nose.

"Smell, Chris."

The dog pointed his snout at the shoes and sniffed away.

"Got it?"

Chris looked up at Hinata, sending the signal that he was ready.

"Let's go, then. Are you coming, too, Mayuka? We're looking for Mr. Takaki."

"Of course!" She quickly slipped on her shoes.

Rinka clapped her hands to her cheeks in flustered panic. "Wh-what should I be doing?"

"Stay here and watch the apartment, Miss Rinka. If we find Mr. Takaki, we'll bring him right back with us."

"A-all right…"

Hinata tugged on the leash and gave Chris the next order. ***"Search!"***

Chris led them down the street, nose pressed to the ground. They passed the police station and crossed at the light, where the signal was already green.

"What is it? Did something happen to Takaki?" Mayuka whispered as they walked.

"That ring belonged to Rui's grandma. I took it to Rui, and he recognized it," Hinata whispered back. They were trying not to distract Chris from the hunt.

But at that, Mayuka couldn't help but raise her voice. "What?! Rui?!"

"Shhh!"

"Oh, sorry… So it was the ring stolen from Miss Sakura-ko's shop?"

Hinata nodded.

"Does that mean Takaki's a jewel thief? That…that can't be right. Can it?"

He wished it wasn't so. But the ring was stolen, and

everyone knew it, so it was hard to believe Takaki hadn't played a role in the theft. The best thing right now would be to find Takaki, convince him to tell the truth, and get him to turn himself in.

Chris led them through the shopping district to the station. If Takaki had taken a train, that would be the end of the scent trail. But it seemed he hadn't. In fact, Chris walked *past* the station and sat down in front of the crossing, where warning bells were clanging.

"I guess Takaki kept going," Mayuka murmured.

The train currently in the station started moving, steadily picking up speed until it was racing past them. Chris watched it go by. Then, once the arms rose, the Shiba Inu got back on the trail and crossed the tracks. From there, the dog continued down the road, then began circling a light post.

"Did the scent die out?" Mayuka said, concerned. Within moments, however, Chris was on the move again. Apparently, the trail was still good.

But after passing a convenience store and turning left, Chris stopped and looked to Hinata for help, whining as his white eyebrows drew together.

"You don't know where to go next...? Wonder if it was another car," Hinata murmured, surveying the area. They were in front of an old four-story building. Homes lined the street to the left and right. There had been people milling about near the station, but it was quiet here.

"What should we do?" Mayuka wondered, looking around for signs of Takaki's spiked hair.

"I guess this is as far as we go," Hinata said with a sigh.

What now? If the trail went cold, they'd just have to take the money hidden at the shrine to Officer Iwata. Or would it be better to bring him to where the money was hidden...?

Meanwhile, Chris suddenly lifted his nose and started sniffing at the air. The tip of his snout bobbed up and down.

"Do you smell something, Chris?" Mayuka asked, bending down to get closer. Hinata put a hand on her shoulder.

"Let Chris work, Mayuka."

The Shiba Inu walked forward, nose still high in the air. He started back toward the train crossing, then turned and faced the convenience store.

There were three parking spots in front of the store. A silver station wagon was stopped in one of them, with its rear toward the street. It was pretty beaten-up, scraped and dented here and there.

Mayuka gasped, grabbed Hinata's arm, and whispered, "Look in the passenger seat!"

Through the rear window of the station wagon, he could see a person sitting in the front passenger seat—the silhouette had spiky hair.

"M-Mr. Takaki!"

Sure enough, Chris was approaching the passenger side of the car. Hinata peered through the window and saw that Takaki was facing forward, looking very tense. The driver's seat was empty, and the key was still in the ignition.

Hinata tapped on the window. Takaki jumped and looked over. His eyes bulged when he saw who it was.

Hinata, he mouthed. Hinata gestured for him to roll down the window. When he did, loud music poured out from inside.

"Hinata, what are you doing here?!" he yelled, just as loud as the music.

The younger boy yelled back, "Mr. Takaki, get out of the car! I want to talk!"

Takaki glanced at the convenience store fearfully, then hissed, "He only went in to buy a drink. Get out of here before he comes back! I have to stay in the car."

"Don't say that! Get out! Miss Rinka's waiting for you."

At the mention of his girlfriend's name, Takaki's face scrunched up. He seemed to be on the verge of tears.

"Please, I'm begging you. Just go away," he said. "I don't want you to get hurt. I just… I can't go back now…"

"Where are you going?"

"…I don't know. Just get outta here…"

He rolled the window back up and put his head in his hands. Hinata was at a loss for what to do until Mayuka tugged on his sleeve.

"Hinata, the back opens on this car. Let's get inside!"

Huh? He was utterly nonplussed. *Is she kidding?*

Mayuka circled around the back of the car and clicked open the hatch. Hinata rushed around after her with Chris. In the back of the car was an old stepladder, some toolboxes, and a large blue tarp, all scrunched up. Mayuka hopped inside and waved for Hinata to join her.

"C'mon, hurry!"

Takaki spun around in his seat and shouted, "Are you crazy?! What are you idiots doing?! Get out!"

"Stay quiet, Takaki!" Mayuka snapped at him. "All of this is your fault in the first place! Hurry up, Hinata!"

Hinata's heart felt ready to explode. Hurry up and do *what*? This, whatever it was, was too much. But Mayuka was already in the back, and he couldn't leave her on her own...

In a panic, he looked at Chris.

The dog had one paw raised as he waited for Hinata's command. Chris was ready to act, if needed.

"G-get in, Chris," he said. The dog hopped into the car, and Hinata followed, pulling down the rear door and shutting it.

"Get out, right now!" demanded Takaki. "Is Chris back there, too?!" The spiky-haired young man was writhing in the front seat. Maybe he wasn't able to freely move his body. Was he tied up? Hinata felt a chill run down his spine.

Mayuka put the blue tarp over Hinata and Chris, then wriggled under it herself. "If you tell anyone about us, you're gonna be in big trouble, Takaki!" she threatened. He went quiet at once.

She leaned against the rear of the back seat, crossed her legs, and held her breath. Hinata sat right next to her and kept his other arm around Chris, holding the dog close.

"Sorry about this, Chris..."

"Don't worry. We're partners, aren't we?" Chris seemed to say as he licked Hinata's hand to reassure him.

In less than five minutes, the driver-side door opened, and the car shifted as someone got inside.

"Want a drink?" a man's voice asked over the loud music. He slammed the door shut, and a seatbelt clicked into place.

"...Nah, I'm good...," Takaki said. It sounded like he was shaking.

"Really?" said the other man. He sounded almost mocking. "Let's go, then. The boss probably isn't happy about the wait."

There was another click as the doors locked.

Uh-oh, we can't get out now. What do we do...? Hinata prodded Mayuka on the shoulder. She elbowed him back.

The car went into a sharp reverse, forcing them to lean forward. The rear of the car swung right; then they felt a thump as it bounced over the curb and reentered the street. Finally, they were off.

Hinata wanted to focus on the car's turns, to follow which direction they were heading. *Let's see—we're moving away from the train crossing outside the station, right?* But after a few turns, he had completely lost his bearings.

The driver started talking loudly. "Your little blunder has really messed things up for us, Takaki!"

Takaki hunched his shoulders guiltily. Mayuka clenched her fingers around Hinata's sleeve.

"I've said it before, and I'll say it again—how the heck did you let the goods get stolen like that? We're out a ton of money because of you."

"I-I'm...I'm sorry..."

Takaki's reply was barely audible over the music.

"Well, *sorry* ain't gonna cut it. That kind of loss isn't somethin' you can make up by just workin' harder."

"I...I know..."

"The boss told me to bring you in, so just stay chill. You should be happy this is an option at all. Usually, we'd just send you to sleep with the fishes."

Hinata heard Mayuka gasp. Then she whispered right into his ear.

"Th-that guy's really bad news..."

It's a little too late to back out now! Hinata thought, glaring at her. This was all Mayuka's idea. And Officer Iwata had warned them, too. *"Don't get yourselves involved in anything dangerous."*

Hinata rubbed Chris's back, silently apologizing.

I'm sorry for getting you wrapped up in this, Chris...

The drive lasted for about thirty minutes or so. Finally, the car thumped over some kind of barrier, then came to a stop as the driver turned off the engine. The loud music died out. Hinata and Mayuka covered their mouths with their hands in the sudden silence.

There was the click of a seatbelt being removed, and the man said, "Let's get you out, then."

He stepped out of the driver's seat first, circled around to the other side of the car, and opened the passenger door. There was more metallic clicking. Takaki had probably been tied to the seat somehow.

"Get out."

The car shifted as Takaki left the vehicle.

Hinata and Mayuka put their heads between their knees, held their breath, and went totally silent.

What will happen to us if they lock the car up? Hinata wondered.

Right at that moment, Chris twitched.

Noticing the motion, Hinata looked over to see a small black dot roaming in through a gap in the blue tarp. What could it be…? *Oh no!*

By the time he realized what it was, it was too late. The black dot approached Chris's snout.

"Yiiipe! Yiiipe!"

Chris shrieked and bolted upright. A spider! The black dot was a tiny spider that had wandered into the car.

"Wh-what the heck?!" the driver shouted from outside. He opened the rear hatch.

In a panic, Chris darted out of the car from under the tarp. The leash slipped out of Hinata's hand. *Chris!*

"What the—?!" the man shouted, stunned. An instant later, the blue tarp covering Hinata and Mayuka was ripped free.

The two of them sat side by side in the trunk area of the station wagon, looking into the menacing face of a very big, scary man. They held their breath and huddled closer together for safety.

"Wh-what are you doing in there…?" he demanded. He was clearly baffled by the unexpected appearance of two children and a dog in the car he'd just been driving.

Takaki came stumbling up behind the man and said, "Um, sorry, sir… They have nothing to do with this. Just let 'em go…"

The man spun around and shouted, "You *know* these kids?!"

"N-no, I don't know them…"

"Then what are they doing here?!" he demanded. As Takaki shrank back and clammed up, the man fixed Hinata and Mayuka with a terrifying glare. "Stay put. I'll be back to deal with you two."

He slammed the door shut and hit the button to lock it.

"Wh-what do we do?" Mayuka asked nervously.

"How should I know? Think for yourself!" Hinata snapped back.

What's happened to Chris? At the moment, Hinata was more worried about the state of his panicked dog than about himself.

"I'm sorry…"

Mayuka rubbed her eyes. She was always full of momentum and excitement at the beginning, but as soon as things went south, it was a different story… If they were going to search for Chris, however, they had to do something before that man came back.

Hinata got up and climbed over the tarp into the back seat, which was littered with plastic bottles and scraps of paper. Was there anything that might help them escape?

His father had once told him that if he were ever in an accident and trapped inside the car, or it drove into a body of water, there was an emergency hammer that could be used to smash open the side or rear window to escape.

Hinata leaned over the gearshift to examine the dashboard and opened the glove box to look for a hammer, but he found nothing. He was just thinking that he should look around under the tarp when the doors of the car abruptly unlocked. Hinata scrambled over the back seat right as the rear door opened again, and he tumbled down next to Mayuka.

"What do you think you're doing?" the large man said again, staring at Hinata, who was now upside down in a heap.

"Umm…"

The boy grunted and sat upright so he could see the man properly. Hinata's father was a former rugby player, but this man was easily 20 percent bigger than him. Although he had a large frame, his facial features were still young. He might have been around Takaki's age.

"Go on—get out," he snapped. "What a waste of my time. Guess I have no choice."

Hinata stumbled out of the car along with Mayuka. Suddenly, the man lifted him up and slung him over his shoulder. The world spun, and Hinata began to feel dizzy. The man's powerful arm was wrapped around Hinata's legs, holding him in place.

"You too," he added, grabbing Mayuka's wrist and pulling.

"Owww!" she yelled. It sounded more like she was protesting than that she was actually hurt, though.

From his upside-down position, Hinata rolled his eyes around, trying to glean information about their location. They were in a desolate parking lot, with cracked asphalt giving way to grass and weeds.

When the man turned, Hinata could see a dry riverbank across the road and, glowing red beyond it, the river itself. It was reflecting the setting sun. Despite the horrible situation, the sight seemed somehow wholesome and familiar.

Where are you, Chris? Hinata's chest stung.

The man took them into a run-down apartment at the back of the lot. Most of the mailboxes lining the entrance were either stuffed with flyers and junk mail or taped shut. It seemed likely that few, if any, of these apartments had proper residents.

The man stopped before the corner apartment on the first floor, let go of Mayuka, and pulled a key from his rear pocket. He deftly opened the door with one hand and pushed Mayuka through.

"Get in there."

He pulled the door shut behind him, attached the chain, then let Hinata down in the entryway. Hinata's head was woozy after being flipped around again, and he crumpled into a sitting position.

"Get up," the man grunted, pulling Hinata by the arm.

A voice from farther back in the room said, "Diamond, bring them back here."

"Yes, sir. Get up—you can leave your shoes on," said the man called Diamond as he pushed Mayuka and Hinata forward.

Although it was dirty and dilapidated, the apartment was otherwise normal. There was a hall past the entryway with doors on the right and left. The right door probably led to the bathroom. The left might have been a bedroom.

At the end of the hall was a joint living and dining room. The floor was dusty, and the table and chairs were arranged haphazardly. There were cardboard boxes stacked here and there, and trash was scattered around the room. The whole place was a mess.

The large sliding door at the far end of the room was blocked by thick curtains, but a strong ray of light peeked through the gap. It must have faced west.

A middle-aged man sat cross-legged on a sofa to the left. He was probably the boss Diamond had mentioned. He had longish white-flecked hair and a sunken face, and he wore a dark suit.

Standing across from him, his back hunched, was Takaki.

"So these are the kids that stowed away in your car," the boss said, glaring at them.

Diamond quickly added, "I'm sorry, sir. I didn't notice they were there…"

"You've all been useless to me today. I'm getting sick of it," the boss said, shaking his head. He jabbed a thumb at Takaki. "You know these kids?"

"N-no, I don't," stammered Takaki, shaking his spiky head. "They have nothing to do with me, and I'm sure they don't know a thing about us, so just—"

The boss raised a hand and shushed Takaki, cutting him off. He clicked his tongue. "I don't care if they've got nothin' to do with this, or with anything. They're here now, so we gotta deal with 'em."

Mayuka clutched Hinata's arm with both hands. He put his own hand on top of hers and squeezed hard.

"Usually, we'd just send you to sleep with the fishes." That's what Diamond had said when they were hiding in the car earlier.

The boss leaned forward, steepling his hands and resting his chin atop them. He stared the children down and said slowly, "Now tell me why you sneaked into that car."

The pair shrank before his withering gaze. Hinata swallowed, but no words came to him. Mayuka was biting her lip, equally silent. All they could do was mentally repeat, over and over, the words Officer Iwata had said to them: *"There's darkness like you'd never imagine in the world of grown-ups."*

I think we might've plunged headfirst into that darkness, Officer Iwata. I wonder what Chris is doing now. Hopefully running to safety… Hinata felt his eyes grow hot.

"Well, whatever… We'll have to check up the ladder to find out what to do with you," said the boss with a sigh. Then he turned to Takaki. "But before that, we gotta talk business. You still need to make up for the loss we suffered on your account. I hope you know it won't be easy. You messed up real bad."

A cold smile spread across the boss's face.

"You got a special little lady, don't you? You can't afford to pull something like that again."

Hinata saw Takaki's hands ball into fists. The young man didn't say anything, however. He just shivered.

"The higher-ups are gonna give you another chance. You'd better make the most of it," the boss said. Then he turned to Diamond. "We're gonna get into the specifics now. You take the brats into the other room and keep an eye on them."

Diamond gave a quick bow, grabbed Hinata and Mayuka by their arms, and started hauling them out of the living room.

At that point, a strange sound came from the front door: *Scratch-scratch, scratch-scratch…scratch-scratch…*

Everyone paused. The air in the room grew suddenly tense.

"What was that?" said the boss, scowling.

Scratch-scratch…scratch-scratch… The sound continued.

"Go and find out," he said, jutting his chin at Diamond. The big man nodded and headed for the door.

All the while, the noise continued. Diamond unhooked the chain with a clatter, then turned the knob to open the door. The scratching abruptly stopped, replaced by the light taps of something prancing away.

Diamond returned to the room, chuckling. "It was the dog, Boss. The dog was scratchin' at the door. It took off right away!"

Chris! Hinata nearly yelped with surprise. Mayuka and Takaki turned to stare at Hinata.

"What dog? What are you talking about?!" drawled the boss, raising an eyebrow.

Diamond hastily bowed in apology. "I'm sorry, Boss. There was a dog in the car with the kids. It jumped out as soon as I opened the back, so I just let it run off."

The boss heaved a big sigh and shook his head. "First kids, now a dog…What kind of circus is this? Forget it. Take 'em outta here."

Diamond pulled the two children back to their feet. Hinata glanced over his shoulder as they left and saw the boss pull a small package out of a briefcase sitting on the sofa.

"Here's the next job's—"

"Woof!"

A dog barked nearby.

"Rrrh, woof, woof! Rrrr-ruff!"

Chris! Hinata smacked Diamond's hand away and rushed back to the living room. Chris was barking right outside the sliding door!

"Woof, woof! Rrr, woof!"

Chris knows we're in here! Hinata felt his heart beat faster.

The boss was clearly annoyed at the loud barking. "Ugh! Diamond," he snapped. "Will you go and shut that stupid mutt up?!"

Diamond strode over to the sliding door and swung the thick curtains open. A huge swath of harsh sunlight came pouring through the exposed glass, causing everyone to shade their eyes with their hands.

The big man slid the door open and shouted, "Shut up! Get outta here!"

It was at that moment, backed by the light of the setting sun, that a dark shadow leaped inside.

Riverside Pursuit

The dark shape landed nimbly on the floor.

It's Chris!

Hinata's heart leaped as he recognized the dog's form against the blinding sun.

The instant Chris touched down, he launched toward the boss where he was seated on the couch, bit the hem of his pants, and started yanking the fabric back and forth, growling.

"Grrr, rrrh!"

"Aaaah! Get off!" the boss yelped, dropping the package.

Hinata bounded across the floor and onto the package, shouting:

"Chris!"

For a split second, he hugged Chris as the dog clung to the man's pants, just long enough to remove the leash still attached to the dog's collar. Then he issued a command.

"Take this and go! Run! Run and don't turn back!"

Chris paused for a moment, then let go of the boss's pants, picked up the package Hinata was pointing at, and darted away. He glanced around the room, eyes sharp.

After a quick look at Hinata, Chris jumped back out the sliding door.

It had all happened so fast.

"What are you doing?!" the boss yelled, once he'd returned to his senses. He kicked Hinata out of his way, then jabbed a hand at Diamond.

"After it! Catch that dog, Diamond! Retrieve the package!"

Diamond's mouth moved in soundless terror.

"B-but I'm so slow..."

The boss's hair was practically standing on end with fury. "Then you'd better get started, you idiot!"

Diamond tried to hurry to the door, but he tripped over his own foot and crashed heavily to the floor.

"Forget it!" the boss fumed, kicking Diamond in a fit of pure rage. "I'll do it myself! Keep an eye on them!"

And with that, he rushed out through the sliding door.

"...Owww..."

Diamond sat up, rubbing his right shoulder where he'd

been kicked. He got to his feet slowly, closed the sliding door, and yanked the curtains shut. Just like that, the room was dark again.

"Are you okay, kid?" Diamond asked, approaching Hinata. Carefully, he sat him upright.

"Y-yeah…," Hinata groaned, holding his side. It hurt, but he was more worried about Chris right now.

"Hinata," Mayuka wailed, clinging to him.

"You know," murmured Diamond, kneeling beside them on the floor, "I ain't got much ground to stand on, considering what I do… But I don't like hurting children. I got a little sister back home about your age."

His big face twisted into something like a smile.

"So you kids just go on and get outta here. I'll figure out the rest. The worst he'll do is yell at me for a while… I hope."

"You should come with us," Mayuka said earnestly. "Do you know about turning yourself in? If you do something bad, you can go to the police and admit what you've done, and they'll give you a lighter sentence. We're here to convince Takaki to do that. That's why we were in your car to begin with!"

Diamond looked stunned for a moment, then laughed loudly. He jabbed his thumb over his shoulder at Takaki, who was still standing there in disbelief. "Guess he had some good friends lookin' out for him. Might be a little too late for me, but… Go on—take him and get outta here."

"But," Mayuka protested, holding on to Diamond's arm.

Hinata spoke up. His voice was hoarse. "Sorry, but I'm going ahead on my own. I have to save Chris from that man. I was the one who told my dog to go, so I have to be the one to rescue him…"

He got to his feet unsteadily and walked toward the sliding door.

When Hinata flung open the curtains, the late-afternoon sun burned his eyes.

He slid the door aside and rushed out into the outdoor air, finding himself on a veranda. A small set of stairs traveled from the railing down to the parking lot below. He rushed down them, raced through the lot, and crossed the street.

Once on the far sidewalk, he looked out over the scene before him—the grassy slope leading down to the river, the path beyond, and the gleaming surface of the water as it reflected the sun. Just like before, he found something familiar and wistful about the sight.

Hinata squinted against the blinding light.

To his right, he could see a man racing, practically tumbling, through the grass. He was already far off. And that meant the rustling in the grass ahead of the man must be Chris.

The Shiba Inu was making a valiant effort, but a dog can run at top speed only for a short period of time. Eventually, the boss was going to catch up…

Hinata jumped into the tall grass, which reached up to his chest, and started running again, pushing the grass aside as he chased after the boss.

I have to save Chris. Chris believed in me and followed my orders. Chris is running through the tall grass, knowing there might be bugs. The thought brought tears to Hinata's eyes. *I can't betray Chris's trust. As Chris's owner, I have to come through for him!*

He was panting heavily. The grass cut his hands as he pushed it aside. He nearly tripped and fell face-first into the dirt.

"Hinata! Let me handle this!" said a loud voice behind him. "This is all my fault anyway! I'll rescue Chris!"

It was Takaki. He had caught up to Hinata. The young man was tall and could take longer strides. He was rapidly closing the gap with his boss.

"Hinata, Mr. Diamond's going to help us, too!" Mayuka called from a distance. Hinata turned to see Diamond racing closer. The momentum of his burly body was almost frightening. Hinata thought he must have been lying when he said he was slow.

"I don't care if it's too late for me! I'm goin', too!" Diamond shouted, passing Hinata.

I'm not alone. The thought filled Hinata's heart with hope. But he didn't stop running. He could sense Mayuka pushing through the grass behind him, too

Up ahead, Takaki was pulling up to his boss. He lunged and wrapped his arms around the man's waist in a full tackle. Even Hinata could clearly hear the older man's roar of fury.

But despite Takaki's best efforts, the other man pried him off and got back to his feet. There was a large rock in his hand now.

Hinata's blood ran cold. *He's going to hurt Takaki with that rock!*

All of Hinata's muscles seized up. He closed his eyes.

"Takakiii!" Mayuka shrieked, now close by. She ran right past Hinata.

I can't do this. I have to open my eyes. With great force of will, Hinata rubbed his face and started running again, chasing after Mayuka.

"Mr. Takaki!" he yelled.

The young man was lying facedown in the grass. Diamond came up to him and knelt down to check on his condition. Mayuka stood nearby, holding her hands together in prayer.

Hinata was once again rooted to the spot. Was Takaki hurt? He felt woozy.

Mayuka bent down, picked something up, and showed it to Hinata.

"Takaki said he had to give you this," she said. "Go, Hinata. The boss is back to chasing after Chris!"

He looked at what she'd given him. "The leash…"

He had taken it off Chris just before the dog ran off. Takaki had brought it with him from the apartment.

Hinata squeezed the leash tight and started running again. The grass was getting taller and taller. Where had they gone? Where was Chris? He hoped the boss hadn't caught up yet…

Through the grass, he could make out the footpath near the river. He pushed his way through and onto the path.

The boss was about nine meters ahead, running unsteadily, silhouetted against the setting sun.

Ahead of him was Chris.

And who was that ahead of Chris…?

Hinata came to a stop. That looked like…

Chris ran straight for the figure ahead, tail wagging furiously, and dropped the package from his mouth into the person's outstretched hand.

"Chris! Is that you, Chris?" the man said, stunned. He petted the heavily panting Shiba.

"Grandpa…," Hinata murmured, unable to believe what he was seeing. It was Grandpa Shunya, walking his three German shepherds.

"There, there, Chris. What are you doing here? And without a leash... What's this?" Shunya said, examining the small package Chris had given him. His gaze traveled upward and down the path—and his eyes went wide. "Hinata...?"

Hinata stood in disbelief.

No wonder this place seemed so familiar. It was the same riverside path he'd come to so many times before with his grandfather while walking the dogs. He just hadn't recognized it because he was facing it from the opposite direction.

"I'll take that back now," said the man standing between Hinata and Shunya, his voice low and menacing.

Hinata returned to his senses. He'd been chasing after the boss.

The man held out his hand and took a step closer to Shunya.

"That belongs to me. The dog took it and ran off with it."

Mystified, Shunya looked from the package in his hand to the man and then to Hinata. Chris circled behind Shunya, keeping an eye on Hinata and the boss.

"Give it here. That dog's a thief."

Hinata clenched the leash in his hand. Flames of fury licked at the insides of his chest.

"That's a lie!"

Hinata shouted, louder than he'd ever shouted before.

"Chris isn't a thief! You're the thief!"

The boss turned back to Hinata in shock.

"You've been stealing from jewelry stores around here, haven't you? Like Sakura Jewelry!" Hinata said, pointing a finger at the package in Shunya's hand. "Open that up, Grandpa. You'll see the evidence inside."

"W-wait," said the boss, turning pale. He started walking toward Shunya but stopped as soon as he noticed the trio of German shepherds growling softly.

Without taking his eyes off the man, Shunya ripped the tape off the package, removed the box inside, and opened the lid. There were a bunch of resealable plastic bags stuffed into it. Shunya took one and held it up to the sun, causing something inside the bag to gleam powerfully in the light.

"A diamond, perhaps...? And it seems like you've got other gemstones in here. Quite a lot, in fact," said Shunya, rifling through the box with his fingers. "If you can't prove that these jewels belong to you, I suppose I'll have to report them to the police as lost articles. They were brought here by a dog, after all."

The boss angrily shook his fist. "That brat gave the package to the dog. He knows it belongs to me."

"Is that right, Hinata?" Shunya asked.

Hinata took a deep breath and tensed, willing himself to be strong. "I handed it to Chris and gave the order to run away. These guys are jewelry thieves, and they were having Mr. Takaki carry their stolen goods!"

"Takaki?"

"The owner of that earbud we found at the shrine. I told you how Chris picked up the item's scent and led us to him, right?"

"Ah yes. Your college-aged friend."

Hinata nodded. "Mr. Takaki started working for them so he could buy his girlfriend a birthday present. But it was all a trap. Mr. Takaki was probably carrying around items for them before he even knew they were stolen. They were having him exchange the goods for money."

He glanced over his shoulder; Mayuka and Takaki were not yet in sight. Hopefully, they were all right…

Despite his concerns, Hinata continued. "Mr. Takaki was given a box like that one. He was told to take it somewhere and exchange it for another package. The other package was filled with stacks of cash. I think that when he realized what the job was, he freaked out and decided to hide the cash and the bag at the shrine. Then he lied to the thieves, saying the bag they'd given him was stolen."

"Lied…?" repeated the boss, scowling.

"Yes, he lied," said Hinata. "But you doubted him, didn't you? You thought Mr. Takaki might have taken the cash and run off with it. That's why you tore up his apartment looking for it. And when you didn't find the money, you stuck that knife into his table!"

Hinata swallowed but kept going.

"That was a threat, wasn't it? You were saying that once he was in on your secret, he was stuck with you for life... We were all really scared when we saw that."

The further Hinata got into the story, the sterner his grandfather's expression became. Still, Hinata continued.

"By coincidence, we found the bag Mr. Takaki hid at the shrine, but we didn't realize what was going on and gave it back to him. He was really shocked. I'm sure it must have been terrifying. If you guys found out he'd lied, who knows what you might have done to him? So the next morning, he hid the bag again, this time in the same place as the cash. And we found that, too..."

"Hinata," Shunya said, fixing his grandson with an exasperated glare. "How could you have gotten involved in something so dangerous...?"

"I'm sorry," Hinata replied, pursing his lips. Now that he thought back on it, they'd made a lot of risky decisions. And even though his grandfather had told him not to, he had made Chris do the work of a police dog. Now Chris was in more danger than ever... Hinata had so much to make up for.

"Hmmm," said Shunya. "And what are you doing here now?"

Hinata stared at Chris, who was peering out from behind his grandfather's legs.

"After that, we learned that Mr. Takaki had a ring that

was stolen from Sakura Jewelry. I thought he must be one of the jewelry thieves, so I went looking for him, hoping to convince him to turn himself in to the police. We found him being taken away in a car, and…"

"You mean you all sneaked into the car on purpose?" the boss said, aghast.

"Yes, we did…," Hinata admitted. "And from your conversations, it was clear Takaki wasn't involved in the jewelry heists. But you threatened him, saying he'd have to work for you forever to pay off the loss you suffered. That was when Chris jumped out and attacked. That's how I was able to pick up the package and order Chris to run away with it…"

Shunya nodded slowly, following along. "I see. There's a logic to everything you're saying, Hinata. You've deduced so much based on the clues you were able to find. So going from what I've heard," he said, gripping the box and narrowing his eyes at the boss, "I clearly can't return this to you. It needs to be brought to the police."

The boss clenched his teeth and closed in on Shunya. "I don't have time to waste listening to this brat. Hand over the package, now."

The grass behind Hinata rustled, and Mayuka shouted, "What? Mr. Shunya?! Oh, I'm so glad! Call an ambulance! Someone's hurt!"

"Mayuka's here, too?!" Shunya exclaimed, dumbfounded. Thankfully, he recovered quickly and lifted the dog leashes to his chest. "All right. I'll make a call at once. But before that…"

He glared at the boss, who backed away, intimidated. Shunya pointed a finger right at the man and gave his dogs a simple order: "Bite!"

The three German shepherds attacked the boss at once. One grabbed the sleeve of his jacket, another his arm, and the third, the hem of his pants.

"Aaaah!"

The boss toppled to the ground, helpless, as Shunya leaped on top of him, immobilizing him at once with a knee to his back.

"Hinata, the leash!" he said, referring to the red leash Hinata had in his hand. Hinata tossed it to him.

Shunya grabbed the leash out of the air with one hand and deftly trussed up the boss's arms and legs. The man was left with his back arched like a shrimp, unable to do anything but lie there on the ground. Shunya quickly grabbed the leashes for his dogs, who were growling at the boss, and got to his feet. Then, after patting the dust off his pants, he pulled a smartphone out of his jacket pocket.

"Hello, emergency services? I've got an injured person here. We need an ambulance…"

Hinata's shoulders slumped as he let out a deep breath. Chris was standing a bit farther down the footpath. The sun had sunk below the horizon, and the sky was now a deep shade of ultramarine. Some stars were beginning to twinkle in the sky.

Chris tilted his head, waiting for some cue. Hinata felt a warmth surge in his chest. He opened his mouth to speak, but his voice caught in his throat and came out strange.

"…Chris, come…"

The dog bounded down the path.

The next moment, Hinata was hugging Chris.

"I'm sorry for putting you through such a scary experience, Chris," he said, resting his chin on Chris's back.

"You did so well, though. Thank you, Chris. Thank you…"

Chris whined sweetly.

Somewhere in the distance, the sound of sirens grew steadily louder…

Homemade Reward

Hinata walked Chris through the shopping district, with a blue leash this time.

Mayuka skipped along beside them, humming a little song of her own making about going on a walk.

After the incident, their parents had grounded them both for a week. They'd been banned from going anywhere but to school when they were out of the house. And after seven whole days, this was their first chance to take Chris out on a walk.

"The blue leash looks good on Chris," Mayuka said happily. They'd used the red leash to tie up the boss, so Yuusuke had given them a blue one from the vet clinic's stock.

The police cars had been the first to show up, before the ambulance. Why, Hinata wondered, had they been so close by, before the crime was even reported…?

Right around the time Hinata and Mayuka hid in the car, Rui had been sitting at home, thinking about what had just happened. Why did Hinata have the stolen ring? Why had he seemed so different from his usual self? These questions weighed on his mind.

In the end, he went to the clinic to tell Hinata's parents. Suzune and Yuusuke were shocked. After peppering Rui with questions, they raced to the police. It was well past time for the kids to come back from their walk, and they were already worried.

Officer Iwata admitted that Hinata and Mayuka had come to ask him about criminals turning themselves in, and that he had been curious why Hinata had gone back and forth outside the police station so many times. The last time he'd seen the children, they were taking Chris into the shopping district. The whole search party decided to go there and ask around.

As a matter of fact, many people had seen the kids. Chris was a rather popular dog around town, it turned out. At last, they found someone who had seen Hinata in the parking lot of the convenience store. The witness had turned to look when they heard loud music coming from a station wagon's open window, and that was when they saw Hinata and Mayuka.

Given that stolen goods were involved and two young

children were missing, the police mobilized. They analyzed the security camera footage from the convenience store, identified the station wagon, and put out an alert.

When Mayuka heard about all of this after the fact, she said, "Wow, the Japanese police really know what they're doing when it counts," as though she were completely uninvolved. It had earned her funny looks from everyone present.

"You were the ones who forced them to do all of this in the first place!" Suzune scolded her. Mayuka shrank back into her chair.

The two professional thieves were arrested, and Takaki was taken away to have his head injury treated in the ambulance that showed up a little later.

According to what Suzune heard from Officer Iwata, he'd required five stitches, but it wasn't life-threatening. Because it was a head injury, however, they had him stay at the hospital, just in case.

"Do you think they'll arrest Takaki?" Mayuka wondered when she was done humming. "Miss Rinka seemed really broken up about it all."

"Once he's recovered, he's supposed to undergo police questioning."

Hinata had a feeling the young man would be found

guilty. According to Yuusuke, simply taking stolen goods from one location to another was a crime called "transportation of stolen property." Although he hadn't known it was stolen at first, the fact that he'd hidden the stash of money was going to be a big problem.

"Oh well… Takaki's not a bad guy, though. Once he's done paying for his crime, we should allow him to pet Chris if he wants. Right, Chris?" she asked the dog, who looked up at her and barked. Mayuka took that as confirmation and flashed Chris a thumbs-up.

"I know I said this once before," Hinata cautioned, "but remember that Mr. Takaki is a lot older than us. He's not just some friend from school."

"I know that!" Mayuka grinned.

There was one mystery that still bothered Hinata, however.

How had Takaki gotten Rui's grandmother's ring? It was the ring that had made Hinata assume Takaki was one of the theives.

"It turns out it wasn't an emerald after all, just colored glass," Rui told Hinata in the waiting room of the veterinary clinic.

When Takaki had lied to the criminals that the entire bag had been stolen, he'd also added a sob story to make it believable: that it was a very important bag his girlfriend had given to him as a present. That didn't convince the boss, of course. But Diamond had slipped him that ring so he could pacify his sweetheart. It didn't have much value to begin with, so the boss wouldn't mind if it went missing.

"But," Rui said, smiling, "my grandma said it's not up to other people to determine the ring's true value... My grandpa gave it to her, and that makes it priceless in her eyes. She even laughed and said maybe he'd been tricked into buying it."

He pushed his glasses back up his nose.

"And thanks to you bringing it back to us, the police were able to find the culprits. She said that only increased its worth."

Hinata smiled back. Hearing that was a big relief.

"Do you think Miss Sakurako is feeling better now?" Mayuka wondered. "I haven't seen her, since I've been grounded. Every time I passed her store on the way to and from school, it was still closed. I'm worried."

"Miss Sakurako is fine. She's doing well," Hinata said. "She was very relieved that the thieves were caught. Maybe she'll even reopen the shop..."

Apparently, knowing that the men who'd broken into her store were in jail had eased some of her fears.

"But even more than that, I'm just happy to hear that

Mrs. Takeuchi's emerald ring came back," Sakurako had said, rubbing her cheek against Latte in the waiting room of Marron Veterinary Clinic.

"Even if it wasn't genuine." Suzune chuckled.

Sakurako shook her head. "No matter what the price tag says, other gems are just products, right? But that was a very special ring to her... I'm so glad it's not lost." Latte licked her cheek as she squealed, "And my son... He says we should reopen the shop! The company where he works as a designer, uh, Chez something—they can turn my store into a franchise. That will make it easier to run the business. They'll provide the inventory and management. I'm thinking about taking them up on the offer..."

"Oh, that sounds like a good deal!" exclaimed Suzune, beaming. "I'm sure it's not always easy, but that store is your reason for living, isn't it?"

She's talking about Chez Bijoux Helen, isn't she? Hinata had thought, recalling its very distinctive and beautiful owner. But...

...Chris hadn't liked that woman.

Or was it just the overpowering scent of her perfume...?

The trio's walk inevitably took them past the police station. From the other side of the street, Officer Iwata waved to them.

"Nice to see you again, Officer!" Mayuka said, rushing up to him. Hinata hurried Chris across the crosswalk.

"I'm glad to see you out and about," Iwata said, examining the three of them with satisfaction.

Mayuka straightened up and gave him a hearty salute. "Reporting for duty, Officer! Thanks to you."

"Thanks to me, huh? Ha-ha-ha…" Iwata reached up to touch his hat, smirking. "You really had me worried, you know that? I'm glad Chris was all right, too. You were quite the hero, weren't you?" he said, crouching to pet Chris on the head. The dog's eyes narrowed with pleasure.

"You bet. A real police dog in action!" Mayuka said excitedly, clasping her hands in front of her chest.

"*Former* police dog," Hinata added hastily. "Remember, Mayuka, Grandpa said Chris won't be going back to the force."

This didn't slow her down, however. "How about 'canine detective,' then? At any rate, he was amazing. I wish you could have seen Chris jumping into the thieves' apartment to rescue us. It was so cool."

"Now, now, Mayuka. Try not to cause trouble again, okay? Everyone was worried about you."

Hinata felt very guilty about the whole thing. "I'm sorry, Officer. But…thank you. I heard you were the one who figured out where we were."

"And *I* heard you solved the entire mystery before the police got there. Your grandpa was bragging about you afterward."

Hinata's entire face went red. "Um, but…they were all just guesses. I didn't have evidence. It was just an explanation that seemed to make sense…"

"I know, but we have a fancy term for that: *circumstantial evidence.* It's not enough on its own, but police often start with just that and use it to find the real evidence."

"Wow, Hinata, good for you!" said Mayuka. "He said you had serkumstansive evidence!" Despite not understanding the word, Mayuka seconded Iwata's praise. Hinata felt himself growing even redder.

"But you still shouldn't put yourself in danger like that," Officer Iwata said, holding up a finger in admonishment. "The jewel thieves have been caught, but there might be more to the case. They could have ties to a larger criminal group, so we have even more careful investigation ahead of us."

Hinata recalled that the boss had mentioned a superior more than once. That probably meant he was part of a larger organization, and the people above him hadn't been caught yet.

Iwata patted Hinata and Mayuka on their shoulders and said, "But the most important thing is your safety. Don't ever forget that."

"Yes, sir!" Mayuka said, beaming. She raised her hand in

the air and swore, "You'll never have to worry about me again. Now, we're going to go finish our walk."

Iwata watched them go, shaking his head and murmuring, "Never, huh…?"

Shunya had let Hinata in on a secret.

"The truth is, Hinata, the case that caused Chris to be separated from his original owner, Mr. Kobayashi, and forced him to retire from being a police dog involved a burglary ring. An international group of jewel thieves, in fact. The incident happened in a port not too far away from here—the same place Takaki was ferrying the stolen jewelry…"

Hinata was stunned. It had never occurred to him that the incident with Takaki might be related to Chris's past.

"As I said before, Chris might be wanted by this organization. Which is why I want you to stay out of trouble," Shunya said with a pained smile. "On the other hand, you and Chris make a good team."

Hinata smiled shyly and blushed. Chris looked back at him and whimpered happily.

"We always wind up around here," Mayuka said with a grin. Their route was taking them toward Takaki's apartment next. "He hasn't come back home yet, right? We can still see his door, though. Let's go."

Why would we want to see his door? Hinata thought. Yet a part of him understood what she meant.

But when Mayuka rushed ahead and peered around the concrete wall at the building, she let out a shriek.

"H-Hinata! It happened again," she stammered, hurrying back to him. Her face was pale. "Another break-in. The d-d-door's wide open…"

What?! Hinata faltered and looked to Chris. The dog's brows were knit with concern.

"G-go and see," she urged him. He had no choice but to take Chris around the corner and up to the building. As Mayuka had said, Takaki's apartment door was wide open.

But when he looked inside, he was filled with relief. He turned back to Mayuka, smiling. "It's all right. It's just Miss Rinka."

"R-really?"

"Well, I've never heard of a burglar wearing thick-soled orange sandals in the middle of a crime," he said, referring to the footwear in the entryway.

Mayuka sneaked up beside him. "D-do those really belong to Miss Rinka?"

Someone came into view on the other side of the doorway.

"Who's there…? Oh! It's Chris and Friends!"

It was Rinka after all. She hopped up and down with delight in the doorway.

"I'm so glad you came over! I have no idea where you two live. I really wanted to talk to you about Takaki, but I didn't know what to do. The police wouldn't tell me how to find you, since it's private information..."

Mayuka was relieved to see Rinka. She put a trembling hand on her chest and said, "Oh, thank goodness... You're all right."

"Huh? Why wouldn't I be?"

"B-because of Takaki...and everything that happened. I thought you would be sad..."

Rinka exhaled. "Yeah, he's a real idiot. Can you believe this? I had to go to the police station to get questioned!" she fumed, pulling on the colorful tie in her hair. "I never dreamed he was going to get me summoned by the police! But I was honest and told them everything I knew, and they realized I had nothing to do with any of it. Later I heard that Takaki completely broke down crying, telling them I didn't know anything and begging them to let me go. If he was going to be that upset about it, he shouldn't have done any of this in the first place..."

They could see the woman's eyes tearing up as she spoke, however.

"And then he got hurt... They said he got hit with a rock while trying to rescue you and Chris, huh? Some hero he turned out to be. In the end, he was the one who needed to be rescued..."

Rinka wiped her tears away, then stood bolt upright and offered them a vigorous bow. "Thank you. Thank you so much!"

"Miss Rinka," said Mayuka, rubbing at her own red eyes.

Tears were streaming down Rinka's face now. "Thanks to you, Takaki was able to get out before he got in too deep. The lawyer said that based on what he did, they might be lenient with him and reduce his sentence to avoid prison time. And he's healing up well. They have him in questioning now. If he gets released, he'll be coming back here."

"He's coming home?" Hinata said, surprised. Rinka used the sleeve of her T-shirt to dry her eyes. Her cheeks were flushed with happiness.

"I don't know yet. I'm just cleaning the place up so that it's ready whenever he gets back."

Hinata felt a warmth in his chest. He was very happy for her.

"Oh!" Rinka suddenly exclaimed.

"What is it?" Mayuka asked. Rinka stuck out her tongue and bonked herself on the head.

"I forgot the cookies…"

"Cookies?" the children repeated.

"Remember when you found Takaki's bag and brought it

back? I promised to bake you some cookies. I'm so sorry. I'll remember to have them ready next time."

Hinata wanted to tell her that it was all right and she didn't need to bother, but Mayuka chirped, "Oooh, I can't wait! You can bring them to the Marron Veterinary Clinic. That's where Hinata's family lives. If you come on a weekday after three o'clock, we'll be home from school."

She's so rude! Hinata thought, flushing, but Rinka gave them the okay sign. Then she leaned over Chris and said, "But you can't have any cookies, even though you did the most work... Sorry about that. What would be a good substitute?"

"Hmm, maybe some jerky would be a nice treat? I think Takaki mentioned something like that before," Mayuka commented, trying to remember. Once again, Hinata was preoccupied with how presumptuous she was being.

Rinka snapped her fingers. "I know! I'm pretty good at crafts, so why don't I make a little Sherlock Holmes hat for Chris? I mean, he figured out where Takaki went. And I bet it would look adorable."

Mayuka's eyes sparkled. "That's perfect!" she exclaimed. "Chris is a talented canine detective, after all!"

"*Woof!*" Chris barked as if to say, "Agreed!"

Even Hinata had to laugh at that.

I bet it'll look just great!

—*The End*—

Afterword

Spending Time with Chris

Hello, all you readers out there!

Thank you so much for opening up *Canine Detective Chris*. I hope that you, like Hinata and Mayuka, become faithful partners of our little hero, Chris...

Chris the Shiba Inu is a very talented police dog who is forced to retire after an unfortunate incident in the field. He is brought to Hinata's family in the hope of finding a fresh start, but a new incident is already unfolding...

Hinata is a thoughtful but shy boy, and Mayuka is a lively, outgoing girl who prefers to act before she thinks. With their help, Chris starts to investigate a case that's popped up in the neighborhood. What's the truth behind the mystery? And who is the real culprit?

Let's talk about police dogs a little. Have you ever seen pictures or videos on TV or on the internet of police dogs being trained?

Police dogs help out law enforcement in a variety of ways. They might use scents remaining at the scene of a crime to track a suspect, or find hidden drugs and explosives, or subdue suspects to help bring them under arrest. Each of these things makes the most of a dog's natural talents, and it's incredible to see them at work.

There are two types of police dogs. First are the dogs raised and trained directly by the police. Second are dogs raised by civilian trainers who can assist the police when needed. In those cases, a dog must pass stringent tests and make it through a police assessment. That was how Chris met the requirements to become a police dog.

Most police dogs are larger breeds like German shepherds and Labradors. But some smaller breeds also meet the requirements. As a Shiba Inu, Chris is considered a smaller breed, but his friendliness and strong bond with Hinata help him achieve all sorts of things.

Believe it or not, your author is more of a cat person. I have a calico cat at home. But for some reason, I just really, really wanted to write a story about a dog, ha-ha. I have to thank my very enthusiastic dog-loving editor for helping me put on the finishing touches. Ms. Kana Muramoto, thank you so much for your strong encouragement.

I must also extend my deepest thanks to KeG, the illustrator who brought this story to life with his wonderful drawings. Although I've never talked to him directly, based on his art, I can tell that he must be a dog person!

I hope you'll follow the continued adventures of Chris, our lovable canine detective!

Tomoko Tabe